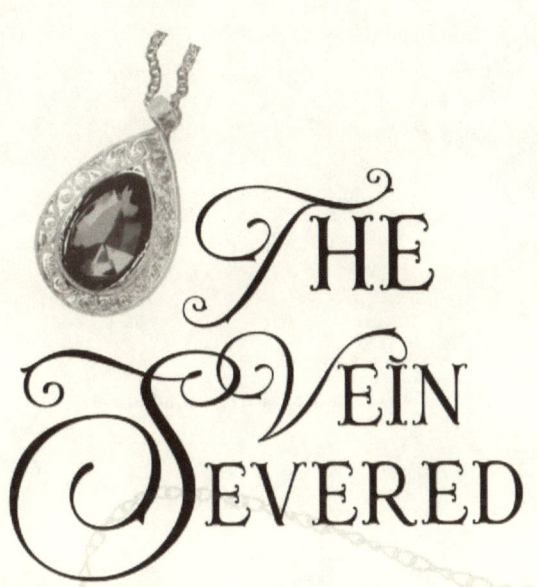

THE VEIN SEVERED

THE VEIN SEVERED

ESTELLE TUDOR

★ ★ ★ ★ ★ ★ ★

Inlustris

First published in the UK in 2025 by Inlustris Publishing, Wales

Text © Estelle Tudor 2025

Cover designed by The Red Fox Creative ©

Interior formatting and design by Inlustris Publishing ©

Edited by Amanda Van Dahm at Prose Perfect Editing ©

No AI used in any part of this publication.

A CIP catalogue record for this book is available from the British Library.

Paperback ISBN 978 1 915950 30 7

E-book ISBN 978 1 915950 31 4

Hardback ISBN 978 1 915950 32 1

"I shall but love thee better after death."

~ *Elizabeth Barrett Browning*

Chapter ONE

Winter, December 1899

I can still smell the blood.

A scent so potent it has a taste. Metallic and cloying at the back of my tongue. Once, it made me retch. Once, it made me so weak I would falter. But still, I force myself to return to this place night after night. Force myself to stay until the sky lightens to a dusky hue, until Lirrel would pull me back to the carriage.

How strange, that the place of my death, would be the singular place that made me feel alive.

On this day, with the snow powdering the ground, I can envision the fallen bodies; splayed out, cloaks twisted like broken wings. Father, Mother, my twin, Nisette...and me ranged over her, protecting her. Doing all I could to stop the monstrous attacker from taking her too. Wielding a fallen branch in my small, white hands, my fear became its own entity, but it was not fear for myself, it was only for gentle Nisette.

At that moment, I did not understand what had happened. How we had been betrayed by our own. How they escaped with the carriage, leaving us at the mercy of something I had no notion could ever exist.

Monstrously beautiful. Dark eyes, pale skin but the smile… oh, the smile. It revealed something far more deadly, far more hideous. Weapons of teeth. Teeth that had severed the lifeline of my parents, and now hunted my sister and I.

Just one taste, beauty…

I close my eyes. No. It could never be just one taste. The greed was insatiable. The need was intense. What the essence craved, became a thing of swift death and eternal damnation.

"My lady?"

My eyes flutter open at the sound of Lirrel's low voice, and for one moment, I am taken back to when he first woke me…the night after I was reborn. Reborn into something unholy, something that should never be allowed to exist.

Drink… you must drink, or you shall die…

But still I linger, regardless of the danger. Feeling reckless, I step closer to the snow-covered road. Scarlet-coloured flecks pepper the pure white of my mind as the memory's fangs sink deep. Reliving the inhuman scream ripping from me as if the last of my humanity fled in the face of something so unfathomable. In that moment, despite that I still lived, I was already dead.

"My lady. Dawn approaches." Lirrel's voice takes on a desperate edge.

"One more moment," I whisper, as red creeps over the navy blue. I have not seen the sunrise in so long. I long to hold out my hand and feel its warmth.

"*My lady,*" Lirrel hisses and grabs at my hand. I have unconsciously lifted it towards those first beckoning rays. He bundles my thick cloak around me and settles the wide hood atop my ebony curls, before ushering me into the dark carriage. He adjusts the heavy black velvet curtains and, within moments, we set off.

The ghosts of my past linger behind us, poised to fade away by dawn's kiss. I wish they would vanish so readily from my mind.

"I do not think you should return here again," Lirrel says, his dark eyes intense on mine. "It is affecting you more the closer we near the…"

I frown and he trails off.

"I have never missed one singular night. I shall not begin now," I reply, my tone as sharp as my teeth.

"But it is different now. You shall be exposed, in danger." Lirrel leans forward, one hand hovering as if to clasp mine.

I entwine mine together on my lap.

"We have always known this day would come, Lirrel. I am resigned to it." My voice loses its bite now, as I lean back against the plush cushions and close my eyes. I force myself to concentrate on the motion of the carriage as we trundle over the deeply rutted road leading back to the manor. Anything to prevent myself from thinking of what will happen when he discovers where I am. What I did.

"We are home." Lirrel's voice rouses me from my near-slumber and I take his hand to alight from the carriage into the barn. I follow him through the covered doorway leading into the manor.

Compelled servants quietly go about their duties, barely looking at us as we traverse the candlelit corridors. Sometimes I wonder if we are the ghosts, or are they?

"You should rest, my lady." Lirrel turns to me at the drawing room door, and I pause in the motion of lowering the hood of my velvet cloak. The deep-purple hue of it is so dark it appears black.

I allow a small smile. "How many times have I reminded you to simply call me Roselle?"

"More times than I can recall, my lady," Lirrel says with a smile of his own.

I incline my head at the futility. "Very well, I shall

see you this evening." I collect a candelabra from the long table in the hallway before making my way up the wide, curved staircase. I feel his gaze upon my back as I ascend.

Inside my chamber, I set down the candlestick and long shadows dance across the walls. I untie the ribbon at my neck and the cloak slithers from my shoulders to pool on the floor. I slip my stockinged feet from the heeled shoes and they join my cloak. Weary now, I do not even bother to undress before I clamber across the cool, silken sheets of my bed.

For these few breathless seconds before slumber claims me, I can almost imagine it is my heartbeat I feel thundering in my ears... but it is not... it is the sands of time, whispering its seductive lure. *Eternity beckons. Death fails.*

I shudder as I succumb to Morpheus' domain...

"Rose... Rose, where are you?" Long, dark, matted hair obscures his face. But still I know it. How could I ever forget his face? Once so beloved, it is now only the source of my grief... and shame.

He pulls against the silver chain, and I wince at the welts at his wrist. His arms are thin and sinewy, caked in a layer of dirt, while his once pristine clothes hang in tatters. But none of that can obscure the loving anguish of his voice. "Rose, please..."

Another voice drowns out his. "Make your choice, Lady Roselle… your sister or… him…"

I am suffocating. I fight my way up, one fist emerging, one slim leg kicking free. I gasp; lungs that need no air still yearn for it. My eyes shoot open, but still I am in the dream, still wrapped up in the past… in the present… in the future that is yet to come, but still so certain.

"Oh, Lorcan." I tremble.

His eyes pierce mine accusingly in my mind.

He is coming for me.

He will soon be free, and I shall have to face what I have done.

One hundred years passed by in the blink of an eye, yet so agonisingly slow. One hundred years of imprisonment. And I put him there.

My husband.

I lurch out of the bed, but my legs will not hold me. I crash to the floor, but I am not granted the retribution of pain. It mocks me in its elusiveness. Instead, I let out a soundless scream.

Lirrel is immediately at my side, drawing me in to his cold embrace. "My lady, my lady," he croons into my hair, holding me as if I am made of feathers and mist. But I am not. I am made of thorns and ash. Deadly and corrupt.

The place where my heart used to be is nothing but a black gaping maw.

I push from Lirrel's hold. I do not deserve his comfort. His loyalty. Not when it was I who sealed his own cousin's fate, for my own selfish wants.

"Please, I need to be alone," I say, letting my long curls hide my face. My hands tremble but I hide them in my lap.

"If you would just drink, this will all go away," Lirrel says in a rough voice and I whip my head to look at him sharply. His handsome, yet slightly pointed, features gleam pale in the low light.

"No. I shall do my penance." *Just as he does his*. I turn my face away, unable to bear the sudden pity in Lirrel's eyes. I do not deserve that emotion either.

"Soon, you will not have a choice." Lirrel stands, his words punctuated by his boots thumping on the stone floor. "You will drink or you will die."

I would rather die…

The words ring hollowly in my mind, an echo of what was, and perhaps what is yet to come.

"I know the conditions," I say through stiff lips.

"Then you know time is running out." Lirrel leans over me, his dark-brown eyes unreadable, yet his tone is plain. He is afraid for me.

Time. What is time? An endless loop or a click of

the fingertips? My memories of certain events have blurred, softened at the edges until I can almost regard them fondly, and with the minimum of pain. But others... others remain in their fractured, blade-sharpened stagnant state. Honed and poised, ready to inflict the greatest amount of damage with the slightest trigger.

I stare up at Lirrel with resignation. "It is not running out, my friend, there is no respite from it," I tell him, and he frowns.

"My lady," he falters, perhaps reading how close I am to the edge.

"Go to bed, Lirrel. We shall speak no more on it." I push myself up, and instantly he takes my hand, helping me stand.

He opens his mouth but, perhaps thinking wisely not to argue, instead nods and steps back, releasing my hand. He smooths back his shoulder-length blonde hair, and I notice his hand shakes. But I cannot allow myself to make a decision for his sake alone.

We each made our own beds and now we must lie in them.

But that kind of rest does not come easy to the restless.

"Sleep well," Lirrel murmurs before backing away. Only when he is at my door does he turn and leave.

I subside onto the bed, pressing a hand to my still chest. There would be no sleep for me now. I dread what awaits me within its cloaked confines. Far better to endure my own company than face my darkest fears again. Once was enough for one night.

I wait a few minutes until I am confident Lirrel has retired to his room, before I make my way out of my chamber and softly pad down the carpeted hallway, the skirts of my long black dress brushing the floor. I choose to only wear muted shades as I mourn my old life. There is no colour in my existence now. No sunshine, no spring blooms, no brightly-coloured gowns. They were as easily erased as I was.

The melancholy is heavy upon me, and so I indulge it. Within the silent library, I pause, my eyes scanning the mahogany bookcases before alighting on the locked chest. I aim for it, my steps purposeful and perhaps not wholly my own. The lure of what it contains is too strong; I crave it now.

With a hand that shakes slightly, I withdraw the locket from beneath the high neck of my gown. I tease open the clasp using one long fingernail and withdraw the tiny ornate key. Before I can question myself, I insert it into the lock, and flip the lid up. Nostalgia, thick and all-encompassing, greets me. I bask in it, a cat arching its back up for one more caress. I bring the withered rose up to my lips, telling myself I can feel its velvet petals and not simply the brittle thorns. Though not its softness, its faint scent still remains, and tears that have no substance threaten. I blink and instead focus on the portrait miniature. Where I had been dark, Nisette had been golden. Sunshine-blonde hair, sky-blue eyes, and petal-pink lips. The summer to my winter.

I trail one reverent finger across the apple of her creamy cheek. I did what I had to do, and I would do it again. I gifted her one hundred years. One hundred years to live, to love, to light up the world. To bear children and for them to grow up.

But now that time has come and gone, and with it Nisette. I became a spectator… a spectre in her life. I haunted her dreams, and lingered on the edges of her days. Watching, observing, ensuring she was safe. But then, as time passed, as it is wont to do, *she* haunted *me*. I watched as she aged, withered away. I stagnated while she decayed.

I allowed her to see me but one time… the night she died. The night she relinquished her borrowed life. A taunting echo of the night *I* died. This time, she smiled at me, her memories of that horrible night compelled from her in the instance of my exchange. She trailed a paper-thin hand across my cheek, thinking I had come to guide her onwards. But how could she know that heaven would forsake me? Only hell awaited. I *was* hell. Yet still she smiled, her blue eyes bright on mine as she breathed her last. And finally, finally, I let her go.

Now, I have a debt to pay.

Life, by its very definition, is for the living. One must never forget that.

So what am I? Just a thief. I, and the others such as I, stole into life, brazenly taking what we should not. What no longer belongs to us. The essence of life syphoned off from those far more deserving.

We are nothing but dark thieves, slipping through the veins of life, like some insidious poison. Life was for the living... so where does that leave us? We have no right to exist, we outstay our welcome lifetimes over, and death—true death—will not look kindly upon our thievery.

A debt must be paid.

One that began with blood and would end with it too. I only hope I will have enough to pay it.

Nisette's portrait flutters back into the chest, and the rose crumples in my convulsing hand. One thorn pricks deep, and thick dark-red blood wells on my thumb, yet I feel no pain.

I allow the blood to gleam enticingly on my skin. I

have trained myself to become numb to its allure. To abstain. Only then could my sister have her life. Only then could her children have a chance.

The blood drips into the chest and lands on another portrait. A scarlet smear against a milk-white neck. My milk-white neck.

A portent of what was… and what is to come.

Time is up.

Chapter Two

"We have a visitor." Lirrel enters my room. The jet stone I was in the process of clasping to my earlobe drops to my dressing table with a clatter.

Lirrel is there in an instant, scooping up the jewellery and carefully clipping it onto my lobe. His fingertips linger for a moment, and our eyes meet in the mirror. I look away.

"Who is it?" I ask, thankful my voice does not quaver.

"Lord and Lady Sorrence's emissary. They seek sanctuary." Lirrel toys with the ribbons and hairpins on my dressing table, and I understand his uneasiness. Lord and Lady Sorrence are part of his family's bloodline. Part of those who embrace the full extent of their dark nature.

"We cannot deny them." My words are statement rather than question, but Lirrel still nods in agreement.

"Indeed. They are permitted one day and one night." This time when our eyes meet in the mirror, I do not look away. We share a look of resignation, tinged with fear. "I shall bid their emissary to escort them in."

"Very well," I say. Lirrel drops the black ribbon he had been playing with and leaves me to finish getting ready for the night.

I lift my mass of black curls and anchor them atop my head with sparkling diamond pins. Lady Sorrence will expect me to appear in perfect poise. She would be reporting back to her master, of that I have no doubt. Her arrival at this precipitous time is not lost on me. A shiver ripples down my spine at the thought, while an echo of a dry mouth ghosts me.

I rebuke the unease and stand to smooth down the front of my deep-purple gown. The skirts are pinned back at the sides, with one ruffle set atop the bustle at the back. The bodice is modest and unadorned, but I indulge in the jet earrings and black beaded shoes. My only concession to the high society lady I once was.

I do not tarry in my room, instead electing to be waiting for our guests when they arrive. I have no wish to allow Lady Sorrence to unsettle me. There will be time enough for that later.

"My lady, you look enchanting." Lirrel offers me a glass as I enter the dining room. I accept it with a gracious incline of my head.

I sip the white wine and wait. The ticking of the

clock appears uncommonly loud, and I wince when it chimes midnight. As if orchestrated, a loud knock comes upon the outer door.

"Do you think it wise to allow Bennett to admit them?" I ask and I watch Lirrel's pale face blanch further.

"You are right. It is most vexing having to find a new butler." Lirrel hastens from the room, and I allow the shudder to leave my body.

Lady Elize Sorrence enters the room, dabbing her mouth daintily with a lace handkerchief. She does not even try to hide the red stains. *Poor Bennett*. Anger flashes through me, but I am quick to temper it.

"My dear, Roselle, what a picture you are. Although, a trifle pale." Elize smiles but it does not reach her ice-blue eyes. She is dressed in the latest style, although the bodice on her bright-red dress is lower than fashionable.

"Elize." I dip my head in greeting. "You look beautiful as always."

She pats her glossy dark-brown ringlets. "You could be as I, if only you would partake, my dear." And so, not yet five minutes in my company, the tempting begins. I should not have expected anything less.

I do not reply, instead I watch Lord Adair Sorrence precede Lirrel into the room. He is dressed all in black, from the top of his long black hair down to the tips of his gleaming black boots. His light-brown eyes rake over me. I do not expect anything less from him either. He has a strangely watchful demeanour; a coiled spring, a serpent ready to strike. He, of all amongst their court, is one I instinctively know to be wary of. He takes my hand and cold seeps into my already frozen bones.

"Lady Roselle. We are most grateful for your sanctuary." A secret smile plays around his thin lips. His gaze is fathomless, and I feel myself falling into it. He blinks and I am released.

I step back and behind Adair, I see Lirrel staring at me, his eyes wide. I give him a reassuring look and offer Adair the standard response. "Sanctuary is granted to those who need it."

"Very prettily done." Adair smiles in approval. His pointed white teeth flash in the candlelight.

I sense Lirrel's relief as he pulls out a chair for Elize. She sits and Adair takes the seat opposite, while I take my usual place at the head. Lirrel pours out glasses of wine for our guests and hands the first to Elize.

She wrinkles her nose. "Do you not have anything… stronger?" Her eyes linger on mine in cruel amusement. "How about your butler? He was *delicious*; tart and mature."

Lirrel rests a hand on my shoulder as he moves around the table, staying my retort. He laughs lightly. "Elize, you know how hard it is to get competent staff. Surely you would not begrudge us ours?"

Adair lifts his wine glass in a toast. "That is sadly true. We have gone through rather a lot of late." His eyes flick over to Elize, who pouts.

"I cannot help it if I awake with a raging thirst. Besides there are always more." She waves an airy hand and, with only the slightest grimace, lifts her wine and drinks.

I barely conceal my own grimace, and when Adair's eyes land on mine, I am thankful he did not notice. He leans forward; the candlelight sharpening the edges of his cheekbones. He stares at me for an uncomfortable amount of time, and I have to settle my hands in my lap less they should betray me. I sense the Sorrences' journey this way, far from their own manor in the south, is significant.

"You have been summoned, my dear," he finally says. Ah, so not simply a prying mission as I suspected, but something far, far more troubling.

Lirrel's fork clatters to his plate and Elize looks over at him with a brittle laugh. "You really must learn to temper your reactions, Lirry darling. It is quite gauche... but then you have been out of touch for too long." She turns her frosty gaze onto me. "But that shall soon be rectified. It is time the *whole* family came back into the fold."

My hands clench in my lap, and she smiles.

"I am sorry you shall have to say goodbye to your century of solitude, but I am sure even you, Rose, must long for company." She picks up her cutlery as one of the footmen brings in a large silver platter. The rare meat runs red and Adair's nostrils flare.

I am delayed from answering while the meat is served. I hold up a hand and the footman continues past me. Instead I heap potatoes and vegetables onto my plate.

"Oh, my poor dear, how disgustingly sad." Elize shakes her head and lifts a dripping piece of veal to her lips.

"It is no hardship," I murmur.

Adair tilts his head at that, inspecting me as if I was some curiosity. "I hardly believed it was true, but you *have* sustained it all these years…" he trails off in bemusement.

"Oh, I cannot wait to witness your full transition. You will be positively feral." Elize spears the air with her fork, her eyes avid on my face.

Lirrel stares from Elize to me, a warning in his gaze. One I do not heed.

"I am afraid you will not be afforded that spectacle," I say, and with slow, deliberate bites I eat the potatoes.

"Oh?" Elize snaps, her gaze darting to a suddenly sharp-eyed Adair.

"Mmm," I say and take my time selecting a baby carrot.

Quick as a viper, Adair's hand strikes out to grasp my wrist. Lirrel half-rises in his chair, but with one look from Elize, he lowers back down. I slowly raise my gaze to Adair. *Do not show fear.* "You. Have. Been. *Summoned.*" He enunciates every word slowly and clearly in his clipped tones.

"I am aware of that," I tell him, and enjoy the way his eyes widen as I finish, "but that does not mean I shall go."

His grip tightens to the point of pain, and with a low growl, he shoves my arm away. "Silly girl. Do you not see? You have no choice."

"That is the second time I have been told that in the space of two days," I muse, resisting the urge to rub my wrist.

"Then you should take note, my dear," Elize snaps. "He is not to be disobeyed."

He. No, *he* would not accept such a snub. I set my cutlery down. I made the deal. I know better than to think I can escape him now.

Adair leans back lazily in his chair. "I thought perhaps it would be Lirrel who would be resistant to the summons, that perhaps he is enjoying this little seclusion too much." He casts an amused look at Lirrel, who stiffens in his seat.

I open my mouth to defend him, but Elize jumps in. "Tsk, tsk, Lirry. Your own cousin's wife." I sit back in my seat. *What does she mean*?

Lirrel does not look at me, but his jaw clenches as he picks up his wine glass and takes a long sip.

"Well, shall we move this along, darling?" Adair waves a hand and Elize's face turns fiercely focused in the blink of an eye.

"Of course. Now where is Bertram?" She stands and claps her hands together. It echoes through the dining room and finally Lirrel gazes at me and we exchange a confused look. After a moment, a shuffling figure enters the room. "I declare, Bertram, I shall drain you dry and leave you staked outside." Elize glares at him.

"Very good, my lady," her emissary says in a monotone. He looks up, and his dark eyes are vacant in his pale face. His dirty light-brown hair hangs in stringy strands to his collar. I am surprised by how unkempt he is. I would have expected the Sorrences' to have higher standards.

"Where is our gift?" Elize asks, a strange smile on her face. Bertram turns and leaves the room.

"No gift is necessary for sanctuary, Elize," I say, but she waves my words away.

"*This* one is," she tells me, and Adair watches me; his gaze hooded.

Bertram returns, but he is not alone. I stand in outrage. With her curled locks, a shade lighter than my black tresses, and her eyes more blue-green than my own green eyes, the girl could almost have been me... a hundred years ago. "What is the meaning of this?"

While Elize giggles to herself, the girl surveys the room, her eyes clearing as she looks at me. "Where am I?" she asks, in a voice that shakes slightly.

I immediately go to her. "What is your name?" I say gently, all while my mind whirls with notions of how to save her from this repeating nightmare.

"Mariette," she whispers.

I smile at her without showing her all my teeth, and position her slightly behind me as I face the others. "Why have you brought Mariette here?"

Elize rolls her eyes. "Goodness, Roselle, you know better than to ask their names. It won't do to get attached to them."

Anger burns through me, and I think of another

time, and of another helpless girl I needed to protect. "I *said*, why did you bring Mariette here?" Even I do not recognise my voice.

"Well, well, well, our Rose has thorns." Adair looks delighted as he stands. I hold my ground, lifting my arms as if I could protect Mariette from his will. "She is merely a gift… a contingency plan, if you will."

Lirrel clears his throat. "Would you care to explain?"

"Allow me, darling," Elize says and Adair bows in acquiescence. "Mariette, be a good girl and come here."

"No," I murmur, but Mariette is already edging around me. The skirts of her pale-pink silk gown rustling as she moves to stand in front of a smiling Elize.

Elize tilts the girl's chin up, exposing the long, pale, column of her throat. "*Delectable*," she whispers, and I see the change in her expression. The sharpening of her gaze.

I did not realise I had even moved, but suddenly Mariette is behind me and Elize is snarling in my face; her fangs elongated. Mariette screams and slumps to the floor.

Adair looks disdainfully at the prone girl and pulls Elize back, away from me. "I think you have made your—ah—*point*," he tells Elize, and she throws him a chagrined look. He focuses on me. "The girl will not be harmed… providing you and Lirrel accompany us home without fuss."

I stare down at the unconscious Mariette, and then back up at the hideous couple. I have no idea if they will keep their word. I have never trusted them, and they in turn leave me alone because of the deal brokered by their master, but that shall soon come to an end. Their knowing looks say it all; I will capitulate. They have orchestrated it that way. They know my story, know what I did in the past. I would do it again, and they know this.

"Very well," I say quietly, and Lirrel looks at me, anguish clear across his face. "But she shall remain with me until we leave."

Elize and Adair exchange a look, and after a moment Elize lifts her shoulder in an elegant shrug. "But of course, as I said, she is a gift." Her smile widens, and a shiver skates down my spine.

There is no such thing as gifts in this cursed life.

Chapter THREE

"I am sorry, my lady. If I'd known—"

I interrupt Lirrel. "What could you have done? Sanctuary must be honoured." I am weary, weary that goes beyond tiredness. I long for this all to be over. I am ready.

"We could have left. Found another place to stay for these final few days."

I laugh, and it is harsh, brittle, to my own ears. "He will always find us, Lirrel. His reach is long, his torment longer."

Lirrel spins away, and in one violent move, his fist is through the wood panelling of my chamber wall, shards flying around me in jagged splinters. I gasp as they slice at my skin. So fast, he is by my side. "My lady, I am sorry." His dark eyes rove over my face, kindling with tiny blood-red embers as he takes in the cuts. My blood must show like livid red veins upon my moon-pale skin. His thumb snakes up, hovering by my cheek.

I whirl away before he can run it over the bleeding fissures. "It is fine," I tell him, my back to him, as I feel the surface cuts slowly heal one by one. Steadier, I turn to him. "Please, ready the carriage."

"You are still going?" Lirrel asks, incredulity taking the place of the sudden tension between us. A tension I have never noticed before... or perhaps have never wanted to acknowledge, until Elize and Adair made mention of it. It was entirely unwelcome to me. Lirrel was my *friend*, my sole companion these near one hundred years.

"Of course. I have never missed one night, you know this." I collect my cloak. "I shall go alone. You must protect Mariette."

Lirrel swallows, refusal in his eyes. I lift my chin, and he turns away. "As you wish, my lady," he says. He casts one swift look at the destroyed panelling before he is gone, his boots clattering on the staircase.

I tie the ribbons of my cloak around my neck and lift the hood, concealing my hair and half my face. I feel the need to shield myself tonight. I glance at the locked door to my dressing room where Mariette slumbers inside. I hope her dreams are not filled with teeth and monsters as mine are wont to do.

Lirrel reappears. "The carriage is ready," he tells me.

"Thank you. Protect her, Lirrel. Protect her as you would me." An unreadable expression haunts his eyes, but he blinks and it is gone.

He bows respectfully, and I move past him, intent on re-visiting my death one final time.

"Thank you, Simpson." My coachman nods at me, his eyes glassy. My meagre staff are never harmed, never fed upon. *Except for Elize and her improper taste of Bennett.* Lirrel merely compels them to believe they work for a normal mistress. They are paid and treated fairly. Lirrel—out of respect for me—feeds only upon animals. And I? I am cursed, but still retain a will to protect those who would else be preyed upon.

Still, I am a monster, perhaps no better than the one who made me. I betrayed my husband, as I was betrayed. My thoughts are bitter company this night. Perhaps, knowing I have come full circle—that the end of the loop beckons—brings some penalty. Or penance. Who am I to cleave the difference?

Stars puncture the velvet sky as the carriage travels across the snow-covered land. I lean out as far as I can and pinpoint the north star. Its constancy has brought me solace these vast years. As the world around me changed, as fashions altered and steam-power competed with horse and cart, two things remained constant. My age—frozen in time at twenty—

and the stars above. We were twinned in the moment of my death. A star burned up, while I froze from within. I look up, as the stars gaze down, and in those crystalline moments, I can forget who I am. What I am. I can once again be the girl I was. The girl who wished upon a star, and had it granted.

I double over in the carriage, echoes of memories leaching my resolve. I wished for love. I *craved* love. And it found me. In the darkest part of the garden, while couples waltzed in the ballroom beyond, a pair of dazzling blue eyes captured me. I fell, fast and bright, like a shooting star knocked from its pedestal, and he caught me. From that moment on, I knew no other, could think of no other. He was mine and I was his. Nothing could rend us asunder.

Until it did.

Until I did.

I dry-retch, tumbling to the carriage floor as it jolts beneath me. *Lorcan*. I cannot think. I cannot move.

I do not know how long I lie on the carpeted carriage floor. I only know that I see the stars through the window, and that they shift and dance. One loses its throne and arcs across the lightening sky, remnants of its crown trailing behind it in golden fragments.

I wish I may… I force myself up, knowing I have wasted enough time. I shall not be back here for a long time… if ever. I must say my goodbyes.

I grip the door handle and push it open, clutching at the door frame for a moment before stepping down onto the snow. It crunches beneath my heeled boot as it compacts. I stagger from the stationary carriage barely noticing Simpson as he slumbers in his seat. The two black carriage horses snort out puffs of air in the still pre-dawn.

I lower the hood of my cloak and icy tendrils caress my neck. I close my eyes for a brief moment, steadying myself. When I am ready, I step across the road to the verge.

Images collide.

Nisette, golden hair fanned around her head like a halo, stares up at me. Her eyes glassy and broken. I remember clutching her to me, and only then did she make a sound. Screaming, pushing me away, staring at me in horror. At the blood staining my neck.

One trembling hand flutters up to my mouth. She saw me for what I was. What I was to become. She saw me seemingly *die*. I did it for her, could she not see that?

Dawn approaches…

Taking his hand had not been the easy choice. I wanted to stay, watch the sun creep over the horizon. To witness it erase the darkness. But I had made a deal… a deal with the devil.

Rose… what is happening?

I did what I had to, I am sorry, Lorcan… so sorry…

In my final moments—after I had been fatally wounded and my parents killed—he had offered me a gift… one hundred untouched years of life for my sister and her line… if I would betray my… my husband. He intended to break him. Turn him into a replica of himself. A monster with a beautiful face.

And I? I had taken the deal. Sealed so many fates with just one exchange of blood. His for mine. Mine for his.

Ripped apart, torn asunder, two hearts cleaved in half. Lorcan imprisoned for one hundred years, and me frozen in stasis for the same amount of time, providing I abstained. To prove the strength of my loyalty to my sister and her kin. I did it, even when I thought I would go insane from the hunger. The thirst. It burned; every fibre of my being enflamed with it until I believed I would crumble to ash. But I needed to endure. For Nisette.

And I had.

For one hundred years.

But tomorrow he would be free and I would have to face my maker. I would have to make another impossible choice… become a monster in truth or die.

I thought I knew what I would do, but now there

is another innocent life hanging in the balance. So many lives. Too many. Am I merely fooling myself that by saving one it will make a difference? Elize is right. There is always more, more who would step up and take their place either willingly or not. I turn away from the verge and return to the carriage. No, I cannot think like that. If I can just save one more, then, it mattered.

I reach inside the carriage and withdraw the dark-red roses I had left there for this final purpose. They have dried out and their petals faded, but it does not dim their beauty. Not even the passage of time can dim a beauty so fine, so exquisite.

With reverent steps, I return, and lay out three roses. Drawing my fingertips across the dried-blood-coloured petals in remembrance.

Father. Mother. Nisette.

I hesitate over the fourth bloom. I do not deserve to be remembered here alongside them. To do so would taint their memory. Instead, I take the flower back to the carriage with me, and hold it like a talisman in my hands. A talisman against wickedness. Against all that would threaten the beauty and serenity of this world. A half-world. Twins of light and darkness, of day and night. I can only exist now in the darkness, but perhaps I can be a shield at the seam of evil and good.

I tap the roof and, after a moment, the carriage sets

off with a jolt. As I close the heavy curtains against the searching fingers of dawn, my last aspect is of three red roses against the pure-white snow, bathed in watery rays of light. My lips curve sadly. I press the final rose to my cheek and close my eyes.

There is no sweeter agony than remembering the ones who have gone on before, knowing that whatever comes after, there will be no reunion. Not for me. They exist far beyond the realms of what my soul will ever be permitted to glimpse.

The rose drops to the floor as a sudden pain lances through my stomach. It burns, *squeezes*, until black dots pinprick my vision. *What is happening?* My fangs lengthen and shorten, unbidden, and my fingers curl convulsively, clawing at my neck.

"My lady... my lady... fight it. You must learn to hold it back. Bury it, lock it so tightly away that it cannot control you. You are in control..."

"It burns, Lirrel, it burnsssss..." The sobs wrack my gaunt frame, until I fear my bones will splinter from the weight of all I carry. The guilt, the shame, the agony.

"It will pass, in time, I promise. I am so sorry, my lady..."

My mouth gapes soundlessly, working against the searing pain, and I fight with everything I have, everything I have learned, and the feeling passes. But the fear remains. The fear of why the sensations… *the raging thirst*… has returned so violently. My undeath sentence is almost up, and with it the conditions that came alongside it are due.

The payment is the fee all of humanity must give at the end of the magnificent gift of life. Death.

But whose death will it be this time? I have already paid in advance.

The carriage door is pulled opened and Lirrel's pale face greets me. I had not known we had even reached the manor.

"Are you well, my lady?" he asks.

I adjust my cloak, and arrange my features into a calm expression. I will not burden my friend with what has just occurred. "I am, thank you," I reply and allow him to assist me from the carriage and into the darkened barn. "How is Mariette?"

Lirrel correctly interprets my real question. "Lord and Lady Sorrence are resting. She is safe."

"Very good, then I recommend we do the same. We have a long journey tonight." I move past him towards the door.

His silence gives me pause. I turn back to see him staring into the carriage at the rose discarded on the floor. Wordlessly, he reaches in and picks it up, slowly bringing it to his lips.

"Lirrel?"

"Hmm?" He turns to me, his eyes full of distraction. "Oh, did you want this?" he asks.

I hesitate, then shake my head. "No, leave it there." I am too full of nostalgia and memories already. My slumber will be restless enough without the addition of the rose scenting my chamber.

Lirrel's hand flexes for a moment and then in a jerky move, he drops the rose onto the seat of the carriage and closes the door. The sound echoes around the barn, and for one moment it sounds like the clanging of a death knell.

Repressing a shudder, I move into the manor, Lirrel close behind me.

"My lady?" Lirrel's voice is tentative, and I pause in the hallway to turn and look at him enquiringly. I notice shadows beneath his dark eyes, and his blonde hair is not so artfully arranged as usual. It hangs loosely back from his face, tied by a black ribbon.

"Yes?" I wait while he seems to gather his thoughts.

"You must prepare yourself for what it will be like. Here you have been protected from the… ah… *debauchery* of our kind." *Not my kind.* "I wish I could promise to protect you from it all, but I am his to command, just as you are."

The words seem to cause Lirrel pain, as if they have barbs on them and slice his throat on the way out. I understand what he is trying to tell me. That if I think I have known horror, then I have been misled. True horror awaits, and I shall be walking willingly towards it. Exposed. Naïve. Innocent to the full extent of what they are capable of.

Going against my own edicts, I reach out and take Lirrel's hand. I search his face. "I shall be on my guard," I tell him. "You have been a good friend to me these long years, Lirrel. I could have not endured it without you."

To my surprise, bitterness flashes across his handsome face. "Do not think me worthier than them," he almost growls. "I have done things you would despise me for."

I swallow, my own throat feeling as though it is coated in shards of glass. "You have proved yourself over and over, there *is* good in you."

He meets my eyes and stares long and hard at me as if he can see what the future holds in my gaze. He drops my hand. "Get some rest," he says and steps back.

I feel a distance growing between us. Perhaps, he is mentally preparing himself for what is to come.

I hope I will be equally as prepared.

But I fear, even if I had a millennia, I still would never be truly prepared.

Chapter FOUR

"Mariette travels with us." I stare Elize down, and a small, amused smile adorns her red lips.

"What care I how the girl travels?" she returns. "The point is that she *arrives* with us all." She lifts the hem of her gown and allows Bertram to assist her up into her burgundy-coloured coach. Two crossed silver daggers above a silver chalice embellish the door of the coach. If I squint, I can see the red droplets dripping from the blades into the cup. It is just like Elize to be so overt in her coat of arms.

"Lady Roselle, we shall follow your carriage. I think it prudent to keep you in sight." Adair offers me his hand and, with little choice but to accept it, I settle my gloved hand into his large pale palm. He walks me over to my black carriage where Lirrel waits with a compelled Mariette. The girl gives me a dazed smile. I know it is for her own safety and to keep her calm, but the whole idea of compulsion still unsettles me. The guilt of allowing it on my own staff has been a constant burden. Lirrel convinced me it was the only way we could move freely, undetected, and unbothered by the locals.

"Lirrel." Adair inclines his head. "No detours please. We are expected." His face sharpens, and Lirrel bows.

"I understand," Lirrel says.

"Very good." Adair relinquishes my hand, and his face is once again the picture of a handsome debonair young man. He bows, and returns to his own carriage.

Lirrel helps Mariette up to the carriage as I take one final look at my family's ancestral home. The turreted manor of dark stone is nothing but a shadow against the clear night sky. But I know it. I can see its outline, follow every crack, every crevice, until it is as though I am tracing them with my fingertips. Every billow of a curtain, every instant of blooms throwing out their dying scent, every whisper of voices is ingrained in my heart, overlayed by deeper memories. Core memories of a past life. When the manor rang with laughter and was suffused in light. Where whispers became song and the staccato of bootsteps became music. That was all before two worlds collided. Before they ricocheted off each other in an explosion of severed, bloodied lines.

Two parallel worlds should never have touched. If

not for me, they never would have. If only I had kept my hand by my side, and not reached out to touch what I should never have coveted. The ripples I caused were insurmountable, and now it is time to pay the price. Again.

I turn away from the now empty manor. I released my staff before the sun set. They are safe in their own homes, with only hazy memories of the mistress who they believe to have gone travelling, and a generous pouchful of coins. Loyalty deserves a reward. I wonder what betrayal deserves?

"Are you ready?" Lirrel asks, and I realise I have been lost in my own thoughts for longer than I ought. Am I ready? It is of no consequence if I am or not. The path had been carved out one hundred years before, and all that is left to do now is to walk upon it, and hopefully avoid the thorns that border the way.

I do not answer, instead I step up into the carriage and settle myself next to a quiet Mariette, while Lirrel sits opposite. I feel the weight of his gaze on my face. The carriage sets off and fancifully I imagine the land exhaling behind us. Now that death has deserted this place, it can return to life once more.

I am restless; my skin tingles and my blood burns with poker-hot surges. I untie the ribbon of my midnight-blue cloak, and shrug it from my shoulders, but still I am aflame. Mariette begins to hum a melody in a distracted way. Despite its softness, it grates across my skin like tiny daggers. I clench the cushions of the bench, my fingernails digging deep. I was wrong. She is no more safe ensconced in here with me, than with the Sorrences'. We are all monsters. The only difficulty is, mine has waited a century to be unleashed.

"Lirrel," I manage, sweat beading the vee of my throat and across my brow. "Protect her."

"Pardon, my lady?" he says, turning from his perusal out of the window.

"*Protect her*," I grind out, my teeth scraping against my lips.

"From whom?" Lirrel leans forward, his eyes widening as he recognises what is happening.

"From… *me*…" I am struggling now, everything I was, everything I used to be, is slowly slipping away. The pain that stabs through me doubles me over.

Lirrel does not go to Mariette, he comes to me, and bands his arms around me, pinning me in place while I buck and writhe beneath him. "Fight it. Fight it like you did before," he urges, but this is different. It is as though the scales that covered my eyes, the chains that bound me, have been removed. I am unleashed.

Mariette, oblivious to the danger she is in, continues to hum, changing it to a lilting tune, and I fight against the hysterical laugh that threatens to burst from me. The battle for her life rages beside her, and her humanity takes shape in the only weapon at her disposal. A tune that I recognise, and once loved. Once danced to. I focus on the memory, and not on the burning within. It is the only chance we both have.

I still, but Lirrel does not yet release me. Wise man. His eyes capture mine, and I am shocked by the stark grief I see in their dark depths.

"It is all right," I tell him, though I am the one who needs reassurance.

He closes his eyes on a shudder, and lowers his forehead to mine. "It is not. It will never be all right again," he whispers.

"Wha—" I begin, but a sudden certainty slams into my mind, one that has me reeling and lurching upwards, bringing Lirrel with me. We tumble to the floor of the carriage. "*He is here,*" I moan.

"Who?" Lirrel says, pushing himself up to look down at me.

Before I can even form an answer, the carriage swerves wildly before shuddering to a stop. The carriage door is wrenched open and a dark figure fills the doorway.

"Remove your hands from my wife." The voice sends delicious, dark ripples through me, but they are soon chased away by a staggering shamefulness.

"*No*," I say, as Lirrel scrabbles off me. Mariette continues to hum, while shouts come from the carriage behind us.

"*Yes*, my love. Miss me?" Lorcan reaches in one large hand. As if I weigh nothing but a handful of petals, he clasps me to him, pulling me from the carriage. His long dark hair hides his face. Hides the expression I know will be displayed upon his handsome angular features. Anger and hurt. An expression he is wholly justified in emoting.

"Lorcan, you cannot do this. You will incur his wrath," Lirrel declares, and Lorcan responds with a growl, so low, so feral, that I feel it viscerally in my bones.

"Do not speak to me," Lorcan spits, and Lirrel's pale face blanches by several degrees more. My husband adjusts me in his arms. The burning within me has ceased to be, instead it is now a strange soft warmth.

In a dream-like state, I watch Lorcan turn his head to look at something behind him, and in the lowlight, beneath his curtain of dark hair, I see his full lips curve into a cruel smile. "Not tonight, Adair," he says, and then we are gone in a blur so fast my head spins, with Lirrel's tortured, "*Roselle!*" echoing in my ears.

Before I succumb to the creeping darkness, I absentmindedly note that was the first time, in the last one hundred years, Lirrel has ever called me by my name...

...The ballroom is stifling, and the shrill laughs of the debutantes' scorch my ears. "If Mama asks, I am in the retiring room," I lean in and whisper to Nisette behind my fan.

"Rose," Nisette chastises. "One of these days you are going to cause a scandal." She raises one perfect golden eyebrow, but a smile twitches at her pink lips.

"Only if I am caught," I say back to her, with a laugh.

I snap my fan closed, ducking around a dancing couple, and make my way along the edge of the ballroom, avoiding eye contact and small talk. I seize an opportune moment and, while Lord Bamford moves in front of me to corner the Earl of Westley, shielding the terrace doors, I slip out and into the heady fragrance of Duke Lamont's vast gardens.

A smile on my lips, I trip lightly down the curved stone steps, enjoying the feel of my dusky-pink skirts against my heated legs. The cool silk soothes them, and I hide behind a tall pillar before lifting my face up to the sky to study the stars above.

"Now that is a pity." A deep, husky voice startles me from my stargazing. I look around, but I cannot see who spoke.

"Who is there?" I say, my voice a breathy whisper.

A figure detaches itself from the shadows of the hedged maze, and my lips part in surprise. A gentleman dressed impeccably in a high-necked white shirt, with matching cravat and a midnight-black jacket and breeches, stares back at me. His bright blue eyes are perfectly framed by hair of deep chocolate-brown.

"Oh," I say, "I did not realise I was not alone."

"Indeed," the gentleman replies, keeping a respectable distance between us.

Curiosity gets the better of me. "What did you mean, that it is a pity?"

He smiles, revealing a flash of white teeth. "Simply that it is a pity that the most enchanting girl at the ball is seeking solace in the garden. Perhaps you find Duke Lamont's entertainment lacking?"

I flush, whether from the compliment or the insinuation of my snubbing the duke's ball, I know not. "Of course not. I was merely overheated, and wished to cool myself." I lift my neck and fan myself with my pale-pink feathered fan. The gentleman watches me with a strange expression. One that disconcerts me and intrigues me in equal measure. I lower my fan. "I should be getting back."

"Stay," the gentleman says, and for one moment I yearn to do exactly that. But instead, I step back.

"I cannot," I tell him, and his eyes widen in surprise. No doubt he is not used to being rebuffed.

"Then promise me a dance, and bequeath me your name. I must know it." His face takes on an intensity.

Exchanging names and promises of a dance with a gentleman I had not been formally introduced to was not the done thing. So, instead, I give a pretty curtsy, one my mother would be proud of—despite the circumstances—and say, "Perhaps, if serendipity allows, you will find me again, and once we have been introduced, the dance shall be yours." Nisette would expire if she could hear my bold statement, but the gentleman inclines his head, an amused tilt to his lips.

"Then I shall wish for nothing more than to find you again," he says.

I smile at him, not the smile of a coy Society miss, but a wide, carefree one. He stills, his eyes capturing mine.

Strange mewling, whimpering sounds coming from within the hedge maze beyond has me looking around, breaking the captivating stare. It sounds like someone in distress. I step forward, fully intent on assisting, but the man blocks my path; a serious look on his face.

"You do not want to go in there," he tells me and, with a deep certainty, I believe him. "Return to the ballroom… where it is safe."

I take in his face, at the force of his blue eyes, and I find myself backing away. My footsteps up the stone steps are quicker than when I had descended. For some unfathomable reason, I no longer wish to be outside. I hurry into the ballroom and welcome the heat and the brightness of the candlelight.

But it is not the gentleman I fear. No, he intrigues me. So much so that I know the exact moment he steps in through the terrace doors. And perhaps he senses me as his gaze arrows in on mine.

He aims for me, straight and true, guests parting to let him through. He is even more striking than I remember. Tall and broad, the candlelight teasing burnished strands from his hair. But it is his eyes, his eyes that hold my attention. Our gazes never waver, not even when my father, who stands beside me, makes the formal introductions.

"Lord Lorcan Lamont, this is my daughter, Miss Roselle Bevingstoke."

A delightful shiver roves up and down my spine as Lord Lamont takes my hand and brings it to his lips. "Charmed," he murmurs, but it is I who is charmed.

Entranced. Enthralled. This man is like no other I have ever met, and belatedly I realise he must be Duke Lamont's son, but I cannot comment on that fact and refer to the conversation that took place in the garden. As far as my father is aware, we have never met.

"Might I be permitted the next dance?" Lord Lamont directs at me, but he turns to look at my father as if seeking his permission.

My father's face is a picture of approval. "Indeed. My Rose is light on her feet, and enjoys dancing." He smiles at me, and I smile back at him before Lord Lamont leads me onto the dance floor, the strains of a lilting tune just beginning.

We join in the cotillon, and as I stare into his eyes, I believe I have finally found the gentleman of my dreams.

How was I to know it was actually the beginning of a nightmare? One that would destroy my whole family, and span the length of perpetuity…

I open my eyes, and realise the true nightmare has only just begun.

Chapter
FIVE

"You are awake."

"They will kill her," I mumble, unable to hide the distress in my tone.

"Hush, that is all in the past." Lorcan moves from the window, and finally I see his full face. He is gaunter than I remember. *All my fault.* But still his bright blue eyes blaze from his handsome face.

"No, you do not understand." I struggle to sit up, and he hovers at the end of the bed. "Mariette. A human girl they brought to ensure my cooperation."

Lorcan mutters an oath and I wince at the savage tone. He notices and takes a step closer, but I scrabble back until I am pressed against the headboard. He stops his advance, a look of such vulnerable grief across his face that I feel it like a blow to my chest.

"There was a time when my presence was not so abhorrent to you," he murmurs, his gaze roving over me.

I am staggered. What did he truly expect? My own

pain and anguish takes over. "You *deceived* me, Lorcan. You supped on your desire to have me until it engorged and consumed what was between us. It overflowed into the darkness, and I was a helpless vessel. I would rather have *died* that night because now... now look at me!"

Lorcan had closed his eyes at the word 'died' and only at my command, did he open his eyes and utter, "I am looking... *You are breathtaking.*"

I cannot stop the sobs now. "No, I am a m—monster." *A monster who betrayed you as you deceived me.* Why is he not condemning me? Why is he staring at me as though he still *loves* me?

I cannot bear it.

I drop my head into my hands and weep until I am gasping.

"Rose, please..." He sits next to me on the bed, and I see him in my dreams, begging me while he is chained up. Chained up because of me. *Rose... Rose, where are you? Rose, please...*

"No. I cannot do this. I must leave." I roll off the bed and back up until I am flush with the door.

He stands slowly. "I am afraid I cannot let you go." I stare at him. He cannot still want me. After what I have done. "It is no longer safe."

For whom? I think, as I remember the incident in the carriage. My laugh is bitter. I know *he* will not stop until he has secured us both. "You do not think you can truly hide me here. *Where* are we?"

Lorcan clasps his hands behind his back as if to stop himself from reaching out to me. "I still have friends, even after all this time. They have provided me—*us*—with sanctuary. And, yes, I hope to hide us here. For now."

"That is a fool's hope," I say, but there is no bite to my tone. I am weary of hiding, of battling my inner demons, of dreading the day when I would have to face my husband. Now that day has come, I fear he is biding his time to exact his revenge. For how else can I explain this inaction, this calmness.

"Then I am but a fool," Lorcan replies, and my stomach clenches at the tenderness in his tone.

I splay my hands against the wooden door behind me, needing the feel of something real beneath my fingertips. I need to anchor myself or I fear I will float away; a dust mote dancing in a wind of unreality.

"I would like to rest," I tell Lorcan, not looking at him. I cannot cope with the depth of emotion within his gaze. It is more painful to experience than my nightmares.

"As you wish." He moves towards me, and I push away from the door and over to the side. He pauses, towering over me. "But do not try to leave, Roselle," he adds in a warning tone, and I give a jerky nod. I do not even know where we are. I would not risk moving about an unfamiliar place in my fragile state.

I cross over to the bed, and lay down, my back towards him. After a long moment, I hear the door open and close. Only then do I press a shaking hand to my mouth, and think of Mariette's plight. I can only hope that Lirrel will do his best to protect her. But I fear I am as big a fool as Lorcan. We are all naught but pawns in a far bigger game. A game that is devised by one who does not play fair. He will find us; of that I have no doubt.

It is only a matter of time.

My dreams are fractured. The past mixes with the present. I linger in the heady days when I would while away countless hours until the nighttime balls. When I would dance in Lorcan's arms, forsaking all others until I almost caused a scandal as Nisette warned. By that point I no longer cared, I was ripe for his plucking. I did not even question a lack of daytime outings. Meeting solely at balls was far more magical in my girlish romantic way of thinking.

I float over the horror of what occurred next, and land back in his embrace as he removed me from the carriage… and I had not even fought against it. So wrapped up in my guilt. So determined to face whatever retribution he wrought. Nisette is long gone. I have done my duty by her. I am fully ready to accept my husband's judgment. But in my dreams, it never comes. Instead, he presses his lips to mine, and I, like a love-starved fool, respond.

But when I awaken again, I discover it is not a dream, but reality, and I am clinging to my husband as though I am drowning and he is my lifeline, my succour. I am ashamed to admit that I continue to kiss him hungrily, despite knowing it is real. Despite knowing that it could be part of some revenge scheme of his orchestrating. But one hundred years is a long time to be denied a lover's embrace. I die in his arms; inch by exquisite inch. If this is my punishment, I will gladly take it.

"*My Rose,*" Lorcan murmurs against my lips, and I know I must withdraw. To continue down this path is folly. Despite my yearning to remain locked in his arms for eternity, it cannot be.

I stiffen in his arms, and pull away. We stare into each other's eyes and I see a shutter come down in his gaze. "I am sorry," I say and sit up. I notice it is still dark. Or dark again? I have no notion of how long I have rested.

"It is I who should apologise. You turned to me in your sleep, and kissed me. I should have resisted." His voice is husky and still has the power to cause shivers to ghost my spine. "But I am still your husband, Rose. Despite the passing of time."

I close my eyes against the surge of pain his words evoke. "Lorcan... I must explain."

"Now is not the time," he says, a slight snap to his words.

"Then when?" I cry, unable to carry the weight of my burden for much longer. I look at him, at the mutinous set of his mouth. "You do not want to hear it... do you?" He does not want to hear the truth of what I did slip from my lips.

"Hear what, Rose? How you spent a *century* with my cousin. When we did not even partake in a honeymoon." The words are dragged from somewhere deep within him and, horrified, I reach out a placating hand to him.

"It wasn't like that..." I trail off as he spears me with his anguished gaze. *Oh, darkness.*

He pushes off the bed, his flowing shirt hanging open at the neck, and strides to the window to stare pensively out of the glass.

Not only had I condemned him to one hundred years of imprisonment, but he believes he was cuckolded. By his own cousin. A sudden, sharp pain lances through my stomach accompanied by the familiar burning. I cry out in pain and tumble from the bed.

Lorcan is by my side in an instant, cradling me in his arms. "What is it, my love?" he asks urgently.

But I cannot speak. My throat is a thousand flaming knives. I clutch at my neck and I see comprehension dawning in Lorcan's eyes.

"You must drink, love," he says and my head whips back and forth in the ferocity of my denial.

I force the words out. "I shall *never*."

"Then how?" Lorcan pushes my curls off my brow and searches my face. He does not know, I realise. He does not know the particulars of the deal I made. And I cannot tell him. Not now. Not when he is holding me so tenderly, so completely, as though revenge is the furthest thing from his mind. How can I spoil this moment?

The burning intensifies and I cannot help the scream that tears through me. I dread it will split me apart. How perfect that I should fracture in my husband's arms, that he should be the one to watch my demise.

The door crashes open, bouncing off the wall, and I sense another hovering over us. His voice seems to come from far away. "What is wrong with her?"

"I do not know," Lorcan replies. "But she is weakening."

I close my eyes as shudders ripple through my body, but the burn subsides. It has passed for now, but Lorcan is right. My strength is leaving me, and I do not think I have much time before I am forced to make the ultimate choice. No... not choice, sacrifice. I am, like Nisette was, on borrowed time.

Lorcan stands and settles me on the bed. I open my eyes and regard the newcomer. He is an older man, with grey hair smoothed back from his forehead. His hazel eyes crinkle kindly at the corners.

"Hello, my lady," he says.

"Hello," I manage.

"This is George, he has offered us sanctuary." Lorcan claps the man on the shoulder and the two exchange a mutual look of respect.

"It is a pleasure to have you both here," George says and I try to summon a smile, but my face refuses my demands. "Can I get you anything?"

"Sweet tea would be welcome," I say quietly, and the two men once again exchange a look, but one of surprise this time.

"Right you are." George recovers quickly, and with a bob of a bow, he leaves the room.

"Tea, love?" Lorcan sits on the foot of the bed, and I am able to achieve a smile. One of sadness. "I do not think that is what you need."

"What I need and what I want are two distinct things," I tell him.

"Is that so?" He watches me steadily, perhaps waiting for me to elaborate, but what can I say? That now I have looked upon him one final time, I can surrender. You win, I want to rage at the universe, you win in this bloody charade. I can no longer play.

I heave a breathless sigh.

Voices out in the hallway have my ears pricking. "She is a danger to us, George," a female voice hisses loudly. "I do not want her here."

"Hush, she will hear you," George replies.

I cast a look at Lorcan, whose lips firm.

George re-enters through the open doorway accompanied by a woman of similar age with faded brown hair. Her grey eyes rake over me in mistrust, as she wipes her hands on an apron.

"My lord, my lady," she says brusquely.

George looks at her sharply, but says to me, setting the tray down and offering me a teacup, "This is my wife, Marta."

I sip the tea, and the sweet warmth works its way through me, fortifying me enough that I can nod and smile at Marta, despite her obvious displeasure of having me as a guest. "Your sanctuary is much appreciated."

She frowns. "Sanctuary is granted to those who need it," she says tightly.

"I have no wish to endanger your family, Marta. I shall not stay long." I set the empty tea cup on the tray and sit up, pleased to note I feel stronger.

"You shall stay as long as you need," George says with a firm look at his wife. She opens her mouth to retort but a feminine voice calls from the hallway.

"Mama?"

Marta casts me a quick look before she curtsies and hurries from the room.

"That is our daughter, Coralie," George says and now I understand Marta's fear. They are hiding runaways, and *he* will take a dim view of that fact.

"Lorcan, we cannot stay here," I tell him.

"It is perfectly safe, no one knows of my connection to George," Lorcan replies in soothing tones.

I shake my head, and George clears his throat. "I shall give you a moment alone." He leaves the room, pulling the door closed behind him.

"Lorcan, that does not matter. I have been *summoned*." I stare at him meaningfully. He, of all of us, should know what that means.

Lorcan's cheekbones sharpen in his gaunt face. His eyes flash with a myriad of emotions. "I will *protect* you," he says in a low voice.

I stare at him. Protect *me*? Did he not see, it was never about me. None of what happened was. It was always about Lorcan. I was but bait, a pawn, and I will not allow myself to continue to be the source of his torment.

"But who will protect you?" I murmur, almost to myself.

He takes an actual step back, his eyes widening. "Rose. This is all my fault."

At that, I surge from the bed, coming to stand before him. "No," I utter and without thinking, take his hands. "You do not understand, you do not know what truly occurred."

His eyes kindle. "I do understand. More than you realise." His voice is harsh, accusing, and I think, here it is, the condemnation, the reckoning, but his next words have me dropping his hands. "But you are my wife, and I *shall* do my duty."

He bows curtly, turns on his heel, and leaves me staring after him.

Chapter Six

I sleep the day away.

As night descends once more, I go in search of Lorcan. He did not return to me, and I need to speak with him. I do not think he truly understands. How could he possibly?

I walk softly down the staircase and find my way into a small sitting room. It is empty and I turn to leave, but find my way barred by Marta.

"My lady, can I help you?" she asks.

I try a friendly smile. "Please, it is just Roselle. I am looking for Lorcan, do you know where he is?"

Her eyes flick away, then back again. "He is in George's study. Wait here. I shall tell him you are looking for him."

"Thank you, Marta," I say, but she merely purses her lips and leaves me. I do not blame her reaction. I, too, resented having to extend sanctuary to all who arrived at my door. Who knew what danger they brought with them.

While I wait I take in the sparsely decorated sitting room, and sit on the faded red loveseat beneath the window. I stare out of the panes and up to the sky; a layer of cloud covers it tonight, blocking out the view of the stars.

"Hello." A soft voice has me turning. A young girl of about sixteen stands in the doorway. Her bright copper hair hangs in coils around her shoulders, some of it pulled away from her face with a yellow ribbon. Her hazel eyes are a match to George's.

"Hello, you must be Coralie," I say.

She smiles and enters the room. She takes a seat opposite me and inspects my face. "Are you feeling better now?" I arch an eyebrow, and she continues in a whisper, "I heard you screaming."

"Oh, of course, yes, thank you, I just have nightmares," I tell her, instead of revealing my screams, this time, were from my sudden burning pangs.

She leans closer to me, her eyes full of empathy. "I do too," she admits. "They never change. For over one hundred years they are the same—"

"Coralie," Marta snaps from the doorway and Coralie jumps to her feet. "Go and help in the kitchen."

Coralie smiles at me, one I return, before she slips past her mother.

"I hope she was not bothering you, my lady? We

65

do not often have… guests." Marta twists her hands together and I know she heard her daughter's words. Words that brought the older woman pain.

"Not at all, she is a delightful young lady," I say, and Marta's face clears, but pain still lingers in her grey eyes.

She nods. "Lord Lorcan will be along presently."

"Thank you."

She nods again, before leaving the room.

I do not have long to linger on Coralie's confession, before every sense in my body snaps to attention. Lorcan enters the room, his eyes on me. He is dressed in a shirt and breeches, but his hair his clean and tied back, and his face looks fuller, though still thinner than it should be.

"I hope you rested well?" he asks, no sign of our previous tension.

"I did," I say. Surprisingly well, considering the circumstances. "And you?"

A bitter smile twists his lips. "I have had all the rest I need for the time being," he says and I wince.

"I met Coralie," I say, desperately trying to change the subject. "She is younger than I thought she would be."

Lorcan takes the seat Coralie recently vacated. He rubs a hand across his pale face. "Indeed. I was the one who found her after… her attack."

"You were?" I say, hating the thought that the lovely young girl had endured the same horror I was all too familiar with. "What happened?"

"You truly want to know?" Lorcan searches my face. At my nod, he continues. "Her aunt was a very willing participant in the gatherings but she was enticed to bring more young ladies with her… and she brought Coralie."

He spoke of the repulsive gatherings where mortals and court creatures mingled. My hand flies up to my mouth, but I need to understand, so I stay quiet as he continues.

"She was so young, not yet sixteen. A line was crossed that night, and I let my feelings be known. Suffice it to say I was punished when I returned from taking her to safety. But it was too late, she had already been reborn. She was fast for a youngling, and I followed her to her home. I was in time to stop her from hurting George and Marta… but once they realised, understood, what had happened to their daughter, they chose to change with her."

"They… they *chose* this life?" I could not fathom it.

Lorcan stares at me. "There are no bounds to what some will do for the person they love."

I sit back. I understand that only too well. But the

truly horrifying dilemma was, what would you do if you had to choose between *two* people you love? The consequences have been my constant companion, and still, I am dealing with the aftermath of that choice.

"Rose. We must talk about what is happening to you. If I did not know better I would say that you are transitioning... but that is not possible after all this time." Lorcan's words bring me out of my melancholic thoughts.

"Then you do not know him as well as you think you do," I say wearily. *I* do not even fully understand how it is possible. That I have lived in a kind of stasis. Neither human nor wholly creature. My full transition stayed until a century had past, as long as I abstained. It was a torture, and agony, all of its own... prolonged, drawn out, to cause the maximum amount of torment. And that was just the physical effects. The burden of knowing I had chosen my sister over my love, and that he was imprisoned because of my choice, added a further layer of pain.

"Then explain. Tell me how I can help you," Lorcan says and I shake my head sadly. I do not deserve his help. I do not even deserve to have these moments of long goodbye with him.

"You cannot release me from this," I whisper. Only I can. But now that I have seen him, feasted upon his beautiful face, I do not know if I am ready to leave him. Selfish creature that I am. We never even had a chance to truly get to know each other. Our romance came on swift wings, not wings made of feathers and down, but of thorns and blood. And I... I had been too blinded by love to see the truth of it.

I blink and Lorcan is kneeling in front of me, his hands on my wrists. "Rose, we have been gifted a second chance. You must see that?"

"Lorcan, we were from two different worlds. We should never have been so presumptuous as to claim even that *first* chance." I cannot look at him now. It is hopeless.

"Do not say that, love. I knew from the first moment I laid eyes on you, that we were destined to be together." His eyes shine impossibly blue in his face, and I waver. I long to lean forward, to take what should not be mine. But I resist.

"We were doomed then, and we are doomed now," I tell him. He still does not know the depth of my betrayal, and I cannot get past his. That it was all a lie. That despite his declarations of believing we were destined, there could never have been a future for us. Destiny played its greatest trick. I do not want this life... and he knows no other.

"No, there has to be a way." Lorcan releases me

and stands. "I *will* find a way."

"It is too late." I stand and look up at him.

"Then I lost after all? You have made your choice?" He stares down at me, and I hate to shatter the last vestiges of his hope, but I must.

I nod slowly.

Pain twists his face into something unrecognisable. "I would have loved you until the world stopped turning," he says, and something within me fractures into tiny glittering shards.

He leaves the room, and I whisper after him, "And I will love you until true death takes me... and beyond."

I know I need to release him from this agony, if it is even half as potent as my own, then he is suffering considerably. Perhaps, George will have a horse I can use. I imagine we cannot be too far away from the manor. It is only fitting my end comes in the place where it all began. I will lash myself to my bed if need be.

I leave the sitting room, and traverse the narrow hallway until I come to a half-open door, and see George sat behind a desk, a ledger in front of him. I tap gently on the door and he looks up.

"Ah, Lady Roselle, please come in." He closes the ledger and smiles at me in welcome. "Do be seated."

I sit in the chair opposite his desk. "Thank you." I wonder how I can broach the subject of my necessary departure.

"I hope you are feeling better?" George asks.

I shake my head. "Unfortunately, there is no cure for what I have—not one I am willing to take," I say, and I watch the understanding flash into his eyes. I lean forward, pressing my point. "I must leave now."

George immediately frowns. "His lordship will not allow it."

I flick my eyes away, gathering myself, before looking at him again. "He does not *need* to allow it. If you have a horse, I can be long gone before the dawn."

"My lady—"

"George, please, your family is not safe if I remain. I have been summoned; he will not stop searching. I owe him a debt."

George blanches, but staunchly shakes his head. "We cannot allow fear to rule us. There will come a night in all our existences when we have to stand against him."

I smile sadly. I once believed that. One hundred years is a long time to plot and plan, but ultimately, I knew it was futile. He is a power one did not merely stand against; he is a power that would obliterate the very thought of it. "I mean no disrespect, George, but

71

standing up for what is right just delays the inevitable. I should know…" I trail off, suddenly bombarded with scenes from my past. The burning returns with a vengeance, and my hands clench on the wooden arms of the chair.

George rises, a torn expression on his face.

"I *must* leave, George… now. Please." I stare at him. "For Lorcan's sake."

"Very well." He scrubs a large hand across his face. "In the stable, you will find horses. Leave the white one—Piren is Coralie's favourite."

"Of course. Could you tell me where we are now?" I will not reveal where I am going but I do not doubt Lorcan will come looking, he feels a duty to our vows.

'Til death us do part…

"We are in Scotland, just over the border," George tells me. So that means I will need to head south, back into Northumberland, and my manor. Not far, thankfully.

"Thank you, George. Please, if you could grant me one final favour and tell Lorcan I am resting?" At his nod, I smile sadly, before standing and offering him my hand. "Goodbye."

George inclines his head as he takes my hand. "Goodbye, my lady." He pauses then adds quietly, "I am sorry this happened to you… to all of us."

I squeeze his hand. "And I you, if there is anything I could do to save you all, I would do it." But we both knew that the truth of it is, we are powerless.

I release his hand, and turn, determined to follow through with my plan before I change my mind. Before the urge to spend my final moments with Lorcan become too much. I leave George's study and after I have walked the length of the corridor to the door, I let myself out into the night.

The clouds break, and the moon shines through, followed by a cluster of stars. They shall be my guiding lights home.

In the stables the horses shy away from me until I talk soothingly and gently. I select one: a pure black mare who regards me without any fear in her soft brown eyes. I saddle her, and mount, running a hand down her silky mane. "Take me home," I whisper, and the horse whickers softly in response.

I nudge her from the stables and walk her quietly away from the dwelling, which I see is a small farmhouse set in wooded grounds, until we are far enough away that her hooves will not be heard.

I cannot resist one final look at the house. "Goodbye, Lorcan. Goodbye, my love," I say, hoping he can forgive me this final abandonment. But this time I do it *for* him. Hoping that when my vacant shell is discovered—which it shall be—that *he*, the one who wields the power, will deem our game over, and leave Lorcan be. I hope my husband can acquire some semblance of peace. He deserves that much. Despite what he is. What I am.

I shake my head in despair, before nudging my ebony steed into a trot along the lane, the way mottled by a leafy fretwork moonlit canopy. I know I cannot linger, but the desire is strong, to stay back the moments of my inevitable demise, by carving out minute instances of pleasure. Of feeling the breeze rippling through my curls, of the crisp scent of the frost being thrown up from beneath the mare's hooves, of basking in the moonlight that caresses my skin... and the memory of my name on Lorcan's lips.

Rose...

"Rose!"

The shout brings me out of my thoughts, and I turn to see another rider gaining on me from the direction of the farmhouse.

"No," I breathe.

Why couldn't he just let me go?

Chapter
SEVEN

"Go back to the house, Lorcan, *please*." I pull up my horse, as Lorcan catches up to me. His hair has come loose from his ribbon and waves around his shoulders, as his blue eyes impale me.

"We are not finished, Roselle." He leans over and takes the reins, but I do not relinquish my hold on them.

"I must go," I tell him. Can he not see the burning stirring within me? If I was to walk barefoot along the frosty ground, the ice would melt beneath me.

"Back to him?" he almost snarls, and I frown.

"Back to who, Lorcan?" He cannot possibly mean the one we hide from, so I search his face in confusion. At what I see displayed there, I recoil in horror. My previous suspicions are confirmed; he does believe I have been untrue to our vows, but still I say, "*No*, you cannot possibly think that I betrayed you in that way?" But I *had* betrayed him, why would he not think that I had gone a step further. Did he think I sought out empty pleasures to ease the passing of the long, lonely years? That while he languished, I was indulging with another.

"Then what would you have me think, wife. You live with another for *one hundred years*, and I am to suppose it was innocent?" The horses step nervously at our heated voices, but my eyes are only on my husband's.

"Lorcan, I cannot blame you for believing I betrayed you, but your accusations in this instance are entirely misplaced. I remain true to our vows." I speak low and try to negate the sound of hurt from my tone. I do not want to go to my end with Lorcan—my only love—believing that I have been unfaithful. There are things I will take to my grave, but not that. Never that.

His blue eyes rake over me, and for one still, silent moment, we are connected. The years fall away and it is like the first time we met. I, with stars in my eyes, and him, impossibly handsome and charming. I almost believe what he had uttered to me in the farmhouse. That we were destined. Are destined. That despite it all, we will find a way.

"Then, if you do not run to him… why do you flee from me?" he asks in a hesitant voice, as if still weighing if my words are true or not. Oh, what a precarious set of scales my words balance on.

"Because…" I press a hand to my throat. "I cannot be what it takes to be with you, Lorcan… and I do not wish to cause you further pain."

He releases my reins to instead cover my hands. "You *can* endure it, Rose. It doesn't have to be the monstrous banquet you believe it to be. The small moral price you will pay to reap the reward of our love would be enough." I turn my head away at his anguished, "*Why* can it not be enough?"

"Because it is not natural, Lorcan. We should have but one life, one true life… and one true death."

"And what of love? Should we not have one all-encompassing *true* love?" He raises my hands from the reins and to his trembling lips and whispers against my skin. "Our love did not die when you did, Rose, and it will endure this too. I cannot lose you. The thought of you, of *this*, was all that kept me going. Please, Roselle."

"You do not understand what you are asking of me. You do not know how I have battled against what I was created for. I cannot allow it to win now. I cannot… I cannot be his *creature*." A sob bursts from me, and Lorcan is reaching over to pull me from the back of my horse to cradle me on his lap.

"You will never be his creature, Rose. Your light still flickers in you, he can never extinguish it. We will find a way. Give me a chance to find it?" He tilts my chin up, and I fight, in a futile battle, against waves of delicious sensation. "*Please*."

Before I realise it, I am nodding in surrender, my resolve fracturing beneath the weight of his obvious love and devotion. In spite of it all, he still loves me, still believes in us. "I will stave it back for as long as I can, Lorcan. But if, in the end, you cannot find a way to free us, then promise me you will let me go? You *must* promise me."

Lorcan closes his eyes, and I miss the blue clarity of his gaze. After a long moment, he raises his lashes and bestows a look upon me so fiercely loving that if I had a heartbeat, it would have stuttered. "I promise," he whispers, "but it will not come to that. I believe I will find a way. I have to."

I should tell him now. Reveal the all of it. Start afresh. But he lowers his mouth to mine, claiming me, branding me, with a searing kiss, and I can do nothing but cling to him and reciprocate with an affirmation of my own.

His lips soften beneath my kiss, and I feel a hint of his fangs as they gently graze my own. It sends a frisson of dark desire straight to my lower stomach, and I hate that, even though that part of him I abhor, it still has the power to disarm my morality, because the rest of him, I *crave*. He makes a noise low in his throat, and runs his hand up my leg, his nails sending electric tingles shooting through me. I arch into his embrace, needing to be closer to him. If not for being on the back of a horse, things would quickly progress to an exquisite conclusion. One that I suddenly need. *La petite mort* beckons, and I moan, vocalising my need.

Lorcan's kiss deepens, and I feel as though his whole being is plunging into me, caress by delicious agonising caress. I welcome it and fear it in equal measure. This loss of control is usually something I deny, but he always had the power to undo me.

In his arms I am undone.

My head drops back in surrender and he kisses along the length of my neck, murmuring my name. I sink my hands into his hair and revel in the feel of the silken strands.

"Come, my love, we must return within the boundary..." he says after what feels like an eternity, and I blink the stars from my eyes.

Before I can ask what 'boundary', a rustle in the trees has the horses spooked. My horse bolts and vanishes back towards the direction of the farmhouse. Lorcan steadies me in his lap, while his own horse circles, its nostrils flaring.

Another rustle comes from the group of trees opposite, and I know with a horrifying certainty that we have been discovered. We led the monsters right to George and his family.

Lorcan stiffens and we meet each other's eyes for one long moment. Anguish in mine, a promise in Lorcan's.

"Isn't this touching." Adair steps from the treeline with an unfamiliar male. "Did you really think you'd get far, Lorcan? I traced your scent for miles, until I lost it right… here." He gestures just beyond us.

"Well, you always were his lapdog," Lorcan returns with a mocking smile.

"Hmm, then why was it you who was leashed?" Adair holds up a thin silver chain and I feel Lorcan tense at the sight of it, as I am still flush against his chest. A bitter taste floods my mouth, as Adair smiles widely. "I suggest you do not run, Lorcan, or else this shall be around your beloved's slender neck before you can blink."

"Try it and you die," Lorcan says.

"Tsk, tsk, gentlemen." From behind us comes the one voice I never wanted to hear again.

I close my eyes at the shiver invading my body, pleading that it is all just a horrible nightmare, but no, it is real, so frighteningly real. A cold hand settles on my thigh, and Lorcan makes a low noise of warning.

"My dear, Roselle, did we not have an

appointment?"

I open my eyes and look directly into the cold, bright-blue-eyed gaze of the duke. Duke Yves Lamont—Lorcan's father. The head of his court... and my creator. I cannot speak, my mouth has fused closed, while my blood burns with an infusion of stinging nettles. I feel the depth of his thrall, pulling at me, pulling at me, but I resist to the point of pain.

"*Stop it*, Father." Lorcan's voice draws the duke's attention to him and I slump against my husband's chest.

"Ah, so the prodigal son returns." Yves stares at Lorcan before looking beyond him thoughtfully. "Clever, very clever. A witch's boundary. No wonder Adair lost your trail after you were released from your confines. My mistake in underestimating you; I should have known your desire to get to her would give you strength. Perhaps, I will not punish him after all." He spares Adair a look, one Adair does not even react to. Threat of punishment is a regular occurrence for members of the duke's court. But still, I shiver as if the words were directed at me.

A thought breaks through and understanding sets in, if I had not tried to leave, we may have remained undiscovered for a while longer. It appears Lorcan has many friends who would assist him. I bite my lip.

Yves returns his attention to Lorcan. "I have no need to discover who or what you shield within." He gestures in the direction of the concealed-to-him farmhouse, and I feel relief trickle through me, until he continues. "You two have now returned. That is all I care about."

His notion of 'caring' is far removed from my own. I am hewn from such a fear, that I believe I will fragment into tiny shards of dust in Lorcan's arms, and be cast to the pre-dawn winds.

"Come, daughter-in-law." Yves spears me once again with his gaze, and I am struck by the likeness between him and Lorcan, but where Lorcan's features are cast with a handsome, otherworldliness, the duke wears his with a sharpened, feral grace. Death lurks behind his eyes, while the promise of eternal damnation sits in the wake of his charming smile. He has not ruled over the British upper class for hundreds—perhaps, thousands—of years without learning how to master his powers, both preternatural, and through his appearance.

He settles his wide hands around my waist and lifts me down to stand before him. I waver, but his grip on me remains. Lorcan is quick to dismount the horse after me and, with a quick motion, he slaps the horse's flanks and sends the trembling equine bolting back towards the safety of the farmhouse, protected by the boundary.

"What did you have to do that for? I was anticipating a good drink," the unknown male says in disappointment.

Yves curls his lip. "You are no better than an animal, debasing yourself to that meagre fare, Draven."

Draven, wisely, does not answer. Instead he bows his dark head, lowering his brown eyes, until Yves returns his attention to Lorcan and I.

"Come now, my children. Dawn approaches and I am keen for our reunion to take place in a far more exalted location. Our family looks forward to welcoming you home."

Not my family. Never my home.

"Father, just let us go. You have had your fun." Lorcan pulls me to his side, and Yves lifts one perfect dark eyebrow.

"Oh, no, my son, the fun is only just beginning." He beckons Adair forward, who comes closer, the silver chain trailing through his fingers. "Now, unless, you want to watch your beloved die now before your eyes, I suggest you come without fuss."

"Trust me," Lorcan whispers into my hair, as he leans down.

Trust me, my love, all will be well. I promise to protect

you. We will find our own way. Our love will sustain us…

Memories batter my mind, while my body is frozen in fear, and I can do naught but stare wide-eyed at Yves. He smiles slowly, fangs gleaming in the moonlight, and then nods in approval.

"Very good. Let us be gone."

Adair and Draven flank us, herding us like cattle, while Yves leans in close. Eyes on me, the world suddenly blurs in a dizzying circle around us, and my only thought is that I shall soon see if Lirrel was able to find a way to protect Mariette.

Darkness knows I could not.

My own fate now rests in the promise of my husband. A husband who is about to find out the depth of my betrayal.

The world tilts as I orientate myself.

I stare at the gothic castle before me, and I cannot prevent the deep shudder that runs through me. I have only been here once before. To the home of Court Lamont.

I wonder now if I will ever leave.

Chapter EIGHT

The last of the moonlight pools over the castle, casting shapes and shadows that stretch out to me like long, accusing fingers, while gruesome gargoyles stare down at me from the battlements; mouths gaping wide. *Your judgement awaits*, they seem to say, and I accept their condemnation.

"Welcome home, my children." Yves rests his hand on my shoulder, the long fingernails grazing my collarbone, and I repress the quiver, knowing it would only delight him to feel my apprehension.

Lorcan takes my hand and squeezes it, and though I know I should feel bolstered by his silent support, I do not. For how can I when I do not know what awaits us. When my husband could very well abandon me to the amusement of those within when he discovers the truth. And who could blame him? I certainly would not.

The heavy black doors are thrown open, and two of Yves' footmen are silhouetted in the doorway. They accept Yves' cloak, and melt away, leaving us to enter.

Standing upon the black-and-red chequered tiled floor, I scan warily around, taking in the vast entrance hall. A wide dark wood table holds two tall candelabra and the flames flicker and dance in an invisible breeze, while many doors lead off from the hall. A curved staircase snakes away from us, observed by countless portraits of Yves and his 'family'. Never-changing portraits despite the years slipping by.

Adair and Draven slot into place behind Lorcan and I, while Yves gestures a lazy hand in invitation to the double doors to our left. I swallow down my distaste. To me it is not a banquet hall but a room of nightmares. The room where my past was erased, and my future altered. With no other choice, Lorcan and I follow Yves into the room.

Numerous members of his court are ranged around the room in various states of repose. Sated by a long night of drinking and debauchery, no doubt. But as soon as they sense Yves' presence, they straighten and rise in fluid movements. After bowing or curtsying, their eyes immediately flick to Lorcan and I. Catlike, cruel smiles adorn many a face, while the whispers and murmuring starts.

I ignore them, seeking out Lirrel, who stands to one side of a throne-like silver chair set upon a dais.

Heavy black brocade tapestries, woven with red and silver thread, hang above. My friend's stoic expression is unreadable, but I notice a tightening of his jaw as he regards Lorcan. Yves wastes no time in taking his seat. His court follow, and sink into their chairs or back down onto the benches of the long mahogany table that runs through the centre of the room, beneath three flickering chandeliers.

"My dear family, is this not an auspicious night?" Yves stares around at his court, and nods approvingly at the rapt expressions. "My son and his lovely wife have returned to us. Returned home." Dark laughter ripples around the room.

Lorcan's grip on my hand tightens, but I cannot look at him. I am frozen. I can feel the sands of the hourglass trickling through the narrow waist, but they become sticky with blood, time smearing across the glass in red smudges of truth. Immobilising this moment itself as judgement day has come.

"Now, where is Elize?" Yves looks around the room.

Elize stands and floats forward. "Here, Your Grace." She sinks into a low curtsy, her red gown shimmering in the light. As she rises, she looks briefly in my direction, her red lips curve in a smile, her eyes hard.

"Where is my son and daughter-in-law's welcome home gift?" Yves smiles in such a way that has my hand convulsing in Lorcan's grip.

"Courage, my love," Lorcan whispers and I wish I could share his.

"I shall just go and get her," Elize trills and, with a swoosh of her gown, she turns and saunters from the room as if she is partaking in a Society ball. *Her*. I cannot simply stand here, for I know who is about to be brought in.

"Lady Roselle? Have you come to take me home?" The sweet soft tones has the burning rippling through me, and I steel myself to meet Mariette's gaze as Elize escorts her in, arm linked through the young lady's.

Mariette is still wearing the dress she was wearing the last time I saw her, but her long dark curls are pulled up into a coil on top of her head, putting her long, slender neck on display. With relief, I note the lack of puncture wounds, but I wonder how long I can keep it that way.

"Lady Roselle?" Mariette says again, and the court laugh mockingly. They know I cannot save her.

I blink and another sweet voice calls to me across the years. The same place, but a different time...

Rose...

Nisette stares up at me. Golden and lovely... but

terrified. She skitters back. Away from my arms, away from me…

"Rose?" Lorcan's voice has me abruptly returning to the present. "Are you well?"

I release my steel-like grip on his hand. For one moment I was still in the past, where Yves' hand was holding mine, anchoring me, cursing me.

I give a minute nod, barely able to meet his concerned gaze.

"Now, where were we?" Yves is now standing, and gesturing for Elize to bring Mariette towards the dais. *What can I do*? My thoughts are in turmoil. "Lady Roselle, do join us," Yves adds in perfect cultured tones.

Lorcan holds me in place next to his side, and now I do look at him. Does he mean to defy his father even now? The duke's plans for his son are far from over. I can see that, even if Lorcan cannot.

"Lorcan, you have become most tiresome. Relinquish your wife, or… I shall make you." Yves smiles pleasantly, but his eyes flash with an imperceptible red gleam.

Eyes on his father, Lorcan tilts up his chin. Then he looks down at me and reverently raises my hand to his lips to brush a kiss on the back of it. My skin tingles. He releases me and steps back. I stare at him, before approaching the dais. I catch Lirrel's eye and the look on his face has me faltering. I have never seen him look so feral, so enraged. He has always worn a polite, unassuming air around me. Which is the real Lirrel?

I step up beside Mariette, and Yves nods at Elize who unlinks her arm from the girl, and resumes her seat.

Yves looks between us, an amused expression on his face. "You do not know, do you?" he asks. At my confused silence, he lets out a delighted low laugh, echoed by his sycophants. It skitters along my spine. "Oh, this is just too diverting." He steps forward and takes Mariette's hand. She has a dazed look about her, and I am thankful that the compulsion has prevented the terror she should be feeling. "Lady Roselle, my dear, I would like you to meet your niece—a few times removed, of course—Mariette Beauchamp."

I stagger back, as though he has struck me. A shrill giggle erupts behind me, but it has sharp edges. As though the fangs cut it on the way out. *Elize*. Oh, how she must have longed for this moment.

No. This cannot be.

I turn devastated eyes upon the duke, but his own eyes dance at his great joke. I am the punchline.

"Well, are you not going to greet her properly? Elize and Adair went to a lot of trouble to secure her. She is this season's incomparable, after all. They took a great risk in luring her, almost from right beneath her betrothed's nose." Yves affects an almost hurt air at my lack of gratitude at this 'gift'. He turns Mariette to face me, tucking her against his side in an almost fatherly manner.

She stares at me trustingly with her blue-green eyes. She believes me her salvation. What if I am her doom? But still, I must try.

"If she is a gift, then she is mine to do with as I see fit, and I demand you return her to her betrothed at once," I say, not even bothering to temper the haughty snap in my tone.

The amusement recedes in Yves' eyes replaced by a warning. "I promised you nothing beyond a century, Roselle. You would do well to remember that."

"Rose?" Lorcan says from behind me, and I flinch. Yves smiles.

"Perhaps my son could do with some company. Adair. Draven," he says. Movement at the back of me has me turning to see Lorcan gripped between the other two males. "There, now we can proceed."

"Let me go, Father. Let us go." Lorcan struggles but he is currently no match for two males who have been free to indulge and retain their strength all these years.

"As I said before… no. Even my own son shall not

disobey me and get away with it. You think you have been punished?" Yves eyes flicker as his fangs flash. "I have not even yet begun."

I cannot help the whimper that sneaks from my parted lips. How can I leave Lorcan now? How can I leave him to eternal torment. And how can I willingly wither away when my own sister's flesh-and-blood is in danger?

"Please, whatever you have planned for them, I will endure it. Release them both and do with me what you will." The words have left my lips before I had even given full thought to them. They take on a will of their own, perhaps incanted from the last sliver of my soul.

Lorcan's shocked, *"Rose, no,"* is drowned out by the murmurs that fill the room. Yves regards me steadily. Intrigue flashes in his eyes.

"Please," I say, fully ready to lower myself to the floor and beg. I have made so many sacrifices. What is but one more? But Yves face hardens as if he can see my intent.

"We do not lower ourselves, we are *royalty*," he hisses. "And it is time my son realises that." With one swift move, almost a blur, he is upon me. *"Drink*, Daughter, or I shall kill your husband." Mariette is thrust against me, her neck exposed, eyes reeling when her enthrallment cuts off abruptly.

The burning begins in vengeance, pain searing through me in a regular staccato; a violent parody of a heartbeat. I force my eyes away from the thumping pulse in Mariette's neck, but still I hear it… feel it.

Can almost taste it.

I battle back the hideous dark temptation and stare mutinously at Yves. "No, he is your son. Your heir. You cannot *kill* him." If that was his plan all along, why delay it one hundred years? For some twisted enjoyment? One hundred years was but a click of the fingers to him, a blink of the eye.

Yves spears me with his blue-eyed gaze as he, once more, reclines languidly on his 'throne'. "He is a *disappointment*," he snarls. "Even his foppish cousin has been of more use to me."

I look to Lirrel, desperately trying to ignore Mariette's whimpering. He stares back, his face paling. "Lirrel?" I ask, but he turns away.

Lorcan, behind me, cries out, "I will *kill* you, Lirrel. You damned snake."

I do not understand what is happening. I glance at Lorcan, who struggles in Adair and Draven's hold, and then back to Lirrel before focusing on an entertained Yves. He watches my face avidly. His own, predator-sharp.

"Lirrel, would you care to tell our lovely Roselle..." Yves trails off, and waves an airy hand invitingly.

"Tell me what?" So much is occurring all at once that I cannot keep up. I am being pummelled by sensation after sensation, but I cannot hear clearly over the roar of my dread, which takes precedence. "*What*, Lirrel?"

Mutely, Lirrel stares at Yves. A sudden stillness overcomes me, the roar receding. "No?" Yves says, and laughs widely, showing his white teeth; his fangs gleaming in the candlelight. "Oh, dear, dear, dear, are you to disappoint me too?"

The ground shifts beneath me; my world fracturing apart. Lirrel is my friend. But I suddenly sense I have been deceived. Horribly and thoroughly. All that I think, all that I presumed to know, is false. I can see it in my friend's eyes.

"Fascinating. Your heart does not beat, yet it can still break," Yves says in a musing tone, as he studies me. "I wonder how many times I can cause it to break, before... *you* break."

I lift my chin, and a surprised glimmer sparkles in Yves' gaze. "You would have made a superior duchess," he says, his eyes roving over me. "Perhaps I was too hasty in marrying you off to my son. Perhaps taking you as bride would have been a worse punishment for him than merely being separated from you." I sense Lorcan still to immobility behind me, his horror palpable.

"I would rather *die*," I utter through stiff lips, and Yves' court hiss in outrage. But I no longer care what happens to me. It was all for nought after all. I allowed my sister a life, her progeny a life, but condemned her descendant to this unspeakable evil... and I am powerless to save her.

I cannot even save myself.

Chapter NINE

Yves surges from his chair and murmurs ripple around the room as he stalks towards me. Lorcan starts struggling once again, and Yves spares him a look, before continuing his progress. I stand my ground, preparing myself.

"Rose," Lorcan says, and I turn to look at him, hoping he can see a century's worth of regret, of apology, in my gaze. Now is the time for him to see it. Know it. I let my gaze linger as Yves stops before me.

"Sleep," he murmurs, and Mariette slumps slowly to the floor, beside me. I tear my eyes from Lorcan's and meet Yves' livid observation. "I think not," he says. "I think keeping you alive—for now—will be far more prudent. I would rather not have to dispose of my son. I would much rather have my heir by my side. But you, lovely Roselle, have shown far more strength, endurance, and devotion to your family, than many of my court. And so, as it appears my son needs more incentive to be persuaded to join me, I shall have to re-think my plans for you both." He trails one long finger down my face, the sharp fingernail scratching my skin. Is he about to reveal our deal to Lorcan? Resigned, I wait. Eyes on me, he speaks to Lirrel instead, "Lirrel, would you like to be rewarded with a gift for your loyalty?"

"Your Grace?" Lirrel says.

With his free hand, Yves reaches down and lifts Mariette as if she is nothing but air and thrusts her in Lirrel's direction. Before she can fall, Lirrel darts forward and catches her. Our eyes meet, and I see Lirrel's throat working, his eyes sharpening.

"No, Lirrel, you promised... promised to protect her as you would me..." I trail off as the room erupts into hysterical raucous laughter.

I glare around at them all in angry confusion.

Yves tilts my chin up, so he is looking deep into my eyes, while Lorcan lets out a low warning noise. "Oh, but my beautiful Roselle... I thought you had worked it out. He *is* protecting her as he did you. That is to say, not at all. He coveted you, understandably, but knew his loyalty was to his court, and so he did what he must." I moan, as I can see everything twisting horribly into shape. Yves continues his almost caressing soliloquy. "It was *he* who told me about you, he who whispered in my ear about you and Lorcan... how my son was in love with a *mortal*, and you, in turn, loved him. It was he who told me where you and your family would be... he who compelled your staff and had them abandon you just as night fell."

"No... you are lying. No... *Lirrel*, tell me it is not true. *Tell me!*" But Lirrel will not look at me now, instead he stands shaking, trembling, as he clutches Mariette to him. A coward faced with the truth. Why will he not *look* at me! Own what he has done, as I should own *my* betrayal to Lorcan. I feel myself pale, the floor beneath my feet undulating in roiling surges. Are we all nought but treacherous monstrosities? Hewn from the lies we tell, and clothed in the secrets we hide.

Lirrel, who I knew in my life before. Lirrel, a charming, elegant gentleman who attended the balls with his genial air and engaging conversation. Lirrel, who befriended me before I even met Lorcan, who danced with both Nisette and I, who never showed any romantic interest in me... or so I believed.

Lirrel, who had comforted me in my first changed moments, by gently revealing what he was to me and that I could endure it as he did. As he *suffered*. What hideous untruths!

The weight of one hundred years crushes me into nothingness. Lirrel, with his lingering looks, attentive care... always by my side. *Why?* Because he had been the spy for Duke Lamont... his master... or because he wanted me, and resented Lorcan marrying me?

Lirrel. It was *his* fault.

Rage and devastation fill my empty stomach. I force myself away from Yves with a strength I did not know I even possessed. I grip Lirrel's face, forcing him to look at me. His expression tells me all I need to know. It *is* all true. Every insidious whisper into the duke's ear, every moment since I met him was just a prelude to this eventuality. But the rest of it? All lies. Lies cloaked in the fabric of friendship. All the times I had allowed him to *hold* me... however briefly. All the times I had needed comforting and he had offered it. I thought in the name of friendship... but he had sought something different. Something more. I retch, my hand clawing at my throat.

I forsook my husband... to spend a *century* with *my* betrayer. It might as well have been Lirrel who had sunk his fangs into my parents, who ripped the very essence of their lives from my and Nisette's existence. He may not have been the executioner, but he was the one who signed their death warrant. A spiteful signature scribed using a quill sharpened to a pointed fang dripping with ink of scarlet blood.

My mind shatters.

I let out an inhuman scream, one to rival the echo

of my death, and fall to my knees; my dark gown billowing out around me as I land. I rock back and forth, screaming, crying, unaware of anything around me. Too caught up in Lirrel's betrayal. I do not know how long I indulge my grief. Perhaps it is the entirety of another century because it does not abate. Will never abate.

"Take her away," I hear Yves say in disgust from far, far away, before I am being grasped and lifted, and carried away. I do not care where to or by whom. I am already in purgatory. Whatever happens next will be a blessed release. Though I do not deserve it. My sins far outweigh those of Lirrel's.

I brought this world to my family. *I* let the darkness smother their light. All because I craved a man and his new and exciting love. Perhaps, I was merely the shadow cast by my family. An omen hovering on the edge. Perhaps, that is all I ever was... all I am ever fated to be.

I close my eyes and finally allow the darkness to claim me. Hoping it will be for perpetuity this time.

But instead I am thrust into the unforgiving past...

...Have I had too much wine? Nisette always did tell me to stick to lemonade. *Nisette. Where was Nisette? Perhaps she is in the retiring room.* I stand in the centre of the room, figures whirling around me in a blur of dark colours and candlelight.

A hand takes mine and, with a dizzy swoop, I step forward. "Come, my dear. I must know you better." The fatherly tone reaches me from far away, but I do not feel afraid at being escorted by a stranger. In fact, strangely, I feeling nothing.

I am deposited in front of a dais and the figure sharpens before me. "Oh, Duke Lamont. Is that you?" I ask, recognising the imposing-yet-handsome gentleman before me.

He smiles a slow smile and I regard his straight white teeth. The little points should disconcert me, but still I feel nothing.

"Father, why have you summoned me? I have business to attend to." Finally, emotion ripples through me at the familiar voice.

I turn, bestowing a brilliant smile on Lorcan. He is dressed somewhat differently to his usual Society attire—in darker and more elaborate clothing, with a red cravat that casts a reddish hue upon his pale skin. His hair is loose and flowing, and I am so caught up in my admiring perusal of him that it takes me a moment to register the horror upon his face.

As he takes a hold of me when I stumble towards him, the duke says, "And is *this* perchance your business?" His voice has taken on a hard edge, but I do not care; my love is here.

"How did you find out about her?" Lorcan stares down at me as he speaks in anguished tones.

"Your eyes," I murmur, noting the red tinge as he looks at my neck, and for one moment I feel a stinging sensation there. I put up a hand slowly and press a hand to my neck, it comes away red. How strange. Lorcan makes a noise and quickly pulls my hair around to cover my neck.

"I discovered your abhorrent predilection for a *mortal* from one who is far more loyal to me. You are my heir... you have a role to play, Lorcan. How dare you defy me!" I flinch at the duke's tone and Lorcan sets me behind him. I clutch at him as the room dances before me. *Where am I? Why can't I remember?* "I want you by my side."

"But a life with her is what *I* want, Father," Lorcan says. My heart is suddenly beating sluggishly in my chest, but I still do not understand what is happening.

"Is that so? You would deny your heritage? Deny everything I have done to bring you into being! For a faux life?"

Lorcan looks down at me, and I see grief warring with resignation. "She is *dying*. If she dies, I will renounce everything!"

I'm dying? Perhaps dying with happiness, I think, wondering why Lorcan is not dancing with me as he promised. He promised to dance with me at my family's ball. Yes, that was it. We were to meet at my family's manor where I hoped Lorcan would ask my father for my hand. We were all in the carriage, on our way to our manor, but the snow was making it slow progress. How had I come to be here? Where *was* here?

My rambling thoughts flitter away as the duke is suddenly before us, but he does not look happy. Perhaps, he does not approve of Lorcan and I. My heart stutters, and I think it is about to stop, but it falters on in a disjointed tempo.

"I think you need a lesson in remembering your place. *Both* of you." The duke takes my hand and Lorcan hisses. "You want her? Then you shall have her," the duke says with a smile, but it only intensifies the brittle harshness in his bright blue eyes.

"What are you going to do?" Lorcan mutters. Is that *fear* in his voice?

Time seems to pass or stand still—I have no notion—but then a shadowy figure joins us and the duke orders, "Marry them."

"What? Father no, not like this," Lorcan says but I am pulled away from my beloved's side.

"You *love* her? You want to *marry* her?" The duke

sneers.

"Yes!" Lorcan says in a wretched, tortured voice.

"And you, my dear. Do you love my son, and wish to marry him?" The teasing, affectionate voice soothes me as I stare deep into the duke's eyes.

"Yes," I breathe. "I wish it to the very depths of my soul... to the very last beat of my heart." The duke lets out a delighted laugh, which seems to echo around the room.

Another voice speaks, but I cannot decipher it, and then I am being thrust towards Lorcan, who clasps me tightly and murmurs into my ear, "Trust me, my love, all will be well. I promise to protect you. We will find our own way. Our love will sustain us."

Protect me?

"It is done." The duke's voice is the last thing I hear before Lorcan is pressing his lips tenderly to mine and I am claimed by shades that reach out inky black hands to wrap around me.

I come around in an extravagant chamber. Heavy swathes of black velvet fabric cloak the bed I am lying on. I feel weak, but clear-headed and everything comes rushing back in... my parents ravaged and splayed on the powdery snow, scarlet speckles flecked across their pale skin as they stare sightlessly up at the sky. I grip the bed post as I stand, nausea pulsing through me.

Nisette! I was protecting her from that... that... monster!

No.

I cannot breathe. I cannot breathe... I cannot bre... I let go of the post and fall to the floor. This cannot be. Things like that do not exist. They *cannot* exist!

I must find Nisette. I must save her.

I pull myself up, and rush across the thick red carpet and drag open the door. Two dark-haired men stand before me, their faces cruel and hungry. I stagger back.

"Don't be afraid, dark beauty," one says.

Just one taste, beauty...

"No, stay back." I look around for anything I can use as a weapon.

The men laugh and enter the room, and a scream readies in my throat. *My throat.* My hand snakes up to feel at my neck and I let out a hiss at the soreness my searching fingers elicit. Oh my god, it was all real. That monster attacked me... I remember the life slipping from me. How am I still alive?

Lorcan! Did I dream he came? None of it makes sense.

"Back." The terse command comes from behind the two—I cannot call them men—and immediately they step away from me, and part. Duke Lamont steps between them. I skitter back, away from him. He is one of them!

He smiles, and bows respectfully. I cannot help but lift my chin at this mocking display.

"My dear, I have a proposition for you." The duke stands with his hands behind his back, his blue eyes dancing in what I can only perceive is amusement. What game is he playing with me? Am I the mouse to his cat?

"I want nothing from you," I say, and he raises one dark eyebrow.

"Impressive for a mortal. So brave, yet I can smell your fear from here." He looks behind him. "Adair, Keir, you would do to take a leaf from this young lady's book."

"Yes, Your Grace," they murmur.

The duke is suddenly before me, clasping my chin in his hand. I had not even seen him move. "Get Valdis," he says, and Adair and Keir leave. My pulse ratchets up and the duke smiles slowly.

"Delightful," he murmurs. He releases my chin, and takes one step back. "I merely wish to offer you a wedding gift."

A wedding gift. Oh my. So I did marry Lorcan. I did not dream it.

"I just wish to go home," I tell him. "That will be

gift enough."

"Oh, but my dear, you shall want *this* gift. I only wonder what you will be willing to pay in return." He walks over to a connecting door and opens it. I follow, apprehension suddenly running like an ice-cold river through my veins. I peer in to the room and let out a gasp. This is no gift, this is but a memento mori... *remember you must die.*

"*Nisette.*" I make to run in and go to her side as she lays asleep on the bed, but the duke's arm snakes out and prevents me.

"Ah, ah, ah."

"What do you want? Let me go to her," I demand, my own fear suddenly forgotten. My sister is alive!

"Now, my dear, I allowed you to marry my son because I believe you love him. But I would like you to prove it."

"P—prove it?" I stumble over my words in my confusion.

"Yes. Choose. Your sister or your husband." The duke waves an airy hand towards my prone sister and then down to my left hand.

Belatedly, I note a ring adorns the third finger. A twisted silver band with a large red stone, so dark it appears black. I stare at it, my mouth drying out. He has presented me with an impossible choice. Surely he knows that. Of course he does. That is why he is so delighted. This is not cat-and-mouse, this is darkness... insidious, devouring darkness, and I am about to fall into it.

Become it.

Chapter
TEN

"What will happen to Lorcan if I choose my sister?" I whisper.

"Mortals." The duke sneers. "I do not know whether to be impressed by your loyalty to your family, or disappointed on my poor, besotted son's behalf. He would have given up all the riches and powers being my son affords... for you. And what will you give up?"

"I want to save them both. I *love* them both!" The words are ripped from me.

"That is not what I am offering you. My leniency only goes so far." He towers over me, cheekbones sharpening, eyes gleaming with a red tinge. So like Lorcan's. *So like Lorcan's.*

No, no, no.

But the truth is undeniable... my new husband is a monster too. How could he ever have thought we could have a future together? He deceived me. Deceived our love. A sob bursts from me, and the duke recoils, yet he tilts his head as if in fascination.

Was any of what I thought Lorcan felt real? Or was

I just a naïve pawn in this charade of everlasting night? The pain of that stark truth strips away the notion of choice. "Nisette. I... I choose my sister," I manage through my tears.

"Very good." The duke runs a hand up my arm, and up to my neck, lingering there painfully for a moment. "Here is what I want in exchange. Your sister and her line shall be safe for one hundred years, but my son shall be punished... and *you*, his new bride, must be the one to do it. For one hundred years he shall be separated from you. One hundred years, he shall have to think on where his loyalties lie. I want him grovelling to be by my side when his imprisonment is over."

"But... but I will be long dead by then," I say, horror and confusion twining themselves around my skittering mind.

"Oh, no, my lovely daughter-in-law. You shall still exist..." he trails off as a gentleman enters the room. "Meet Valdis, my necromancer." I stare at the tall, slender, white-haired man, dressed in black robes embroidered with a red swirling design on the cuffs and neck. Valdis inclines his head solemnly, his pale blue eyes eerily expressionless. "His assistant stopped your imminent death so we could have this talk and you could make your choice."

I think of how I thought I had died by that

monster's attack. The one that killed my parents, of how woozy I felt when marrying Lorcan. I had been near death then, but in reality I had been dead the minute my parents, Nisette, and I had been set upon. Roselle had died in the snow, and this, whatever I was or was about to become was just a shadow of that girl. Decanted darkness in human form.

"Valdis shall perform a spell, one that shall link you and my son, using this." He holds up a thin silver chain. "I will change you, and Valdis and his assistant has concocted a potion that will ensure your—ah—survival. It will sustain you for one hundred years." He stares at me. "However, it will not stave off the thirst. *That* will be down to you, and how determined you are to ensure your sister's continued protection. If you partake, you forfeit our deal, and *I*" — he takes my face in his hand, forcing my eyes up — "I will take *great* delight in draining every last single member of what is left of your family." He smiles, revealing his fangs, at my gasp. So, I was to be punished too for daring to love his son. Coerced into a monstrous half-life, knowing my beloved suffered because of me... my sister and her line hanging in a balance, with my ability to endure the deciding factor.

"I—I understand," I say. The choice is merely an illusion. I have no choice really. At least by doing this, by freeing Nisette, Lorcan will still continue to exist. I convince myself I am doing the noble thing by giving them both a chance at a future. But oh, how I hate myself for betraying Lorcan. Despite him hiding a terrible secret from me, I still cannot reconcile to my own deception. I am just as vile as the duke. Toying with the futures of those I purported to care about.

"Go, say your goodbyes." The duke moves away from the doorway as Nisette moans on the bed. I wonder at his sudden benevolence. But this, too, is a kind of torture. Knowing I shall never see her again. Never talk freely with her, or giggle in alcoves at crowded balls. Never see her fall in love.

I rush over to the bed.

Nisette blinks up at me. Golden and lovely… but terrified, oh, so terrified. She scrabbles back. Away from my arms, away from me. She can see I am changed. Not yet in truth, but it hovers over me like a mask readying to slip over my features. "What is happening, Rose?" Her eyes latch onto my neck. "What has happened to you? I want to go home."

"Of course, my darling. You can go home." I bite back the sob. "Go to Aunt Sara. You will be safe there…" The sobs best me.

"But… what about you, Rose. Are you not coming too?" Despite the blood staining my neck and Nisette's obvious fear of the alteration in me—perhaps, seeing what I am soon to become—she *still* wants me to go with her.

"I cannot, Nis." I manage.

"You must! I shall not leave here without you." Strength returns to my sister's voice, and I stare at her animated, yet delicate features, branding them to my memory. Holding them safe within the confines of my shattering mind.

"That is enough." The duke joins me and despite his promises, I still want to shield my sister from him. I know what I have just condemned myself to—what I have condemned Lorcan to—but still I believe I can stave it back, even now. He looks at Nisette, his eyes flickering with greed, and I turn away from my fear, fully ready to step between them, and force him to seal the pact now. But he does not touch my sister. He merely leans around me and looks deep into her eyes and whispers in a slow, mesmeric voice, "You shall not remember any of this. Your parents and sister were slain in an animal attack, and you survived. If asked, you cannot recall the details. You will be safe." Now, he looks at me. "So long as you keep to your end of the bargain."

I swallow. "I vow it."

The duke nods, then in one swift move, places a

hand on Nisette. "Sleep." She crumples back onto the bed, and I take a moment to press a kiss to her forehead.

"Goodbye, Nisette. Be happy." I turn to find the duke watching me, his head tilted in thought, as if I am some unknown specimen to dissect. "Promise me, she will be safe. Promise me!" I say to him.

He lifts one shoulder nonchalantly. "It can be no other way. Once the pact is sealed—once it is bound by blood magic—it cannot be undone by me... unless you renege."

My eyes on Nisette now, I murmur, "I shall do what must be done to ensure her safety." I close my eyes against the horror and terror that suddenly swamps me. But acutely aware of my sister's gentle breathing behind me, I open my eyes, fully prepared for my own breathing to cease to be.

All it will take is one exchange of blood, an incantation... and a betrayal...

The duke leads me from Nisette's room, and closes the door behind us. My heart begins to dance in my chest and the duke spears me with a glance from beneath hooded eyes. We traverse long corridors and up into a tower. If the duke was not holding onto me, I feel I would float away. My mind is detaching itself from my body, and I embrace it. It is far better than the fear that wants to envelop me.

At the top of the tower is a room lined with many shelves holding glass vials, specimen jars and books. Valdis directs us to the centre of the room. I sink onto the chaise there while he readies a silver goblet. I watch, separate from everything going on inside me, while the duke allows Valdis to pierce his thumb with the point of a dagger. Scarlet droplets drip into the goblet.

As one, the males turn, Valdis, goblet in hand, the duke, fangs bared. I gasp but the duke is upon me, searing open the recently closed wounds on my neck, and drinks deep, deep, deeper still. I do not cry out. My eyes flutter closed and I succumb, hanging loose in his deathly embrace. This, is no more than I deserve. "Welcome to the family, daughter-in-law," the duke utters against my neck.

My heart beat falters. Beat... bea...be.............
....
..........................b...

A hand cups the back of my head, and a goblet is pressed to my lips. Instinctively I drink, gagging on the bitter, metallic taste.

"All of it, my dear," a voice croons. The duke's voice. The creator of the monster I am to become.

I swallow it all, despite the gagging sensation in

my throat.

Immediately, a burning pain rips through my whole body as though my skin is not made for me. I want to shed it. The pain recedes but another one mercilessly follows it—this time in my jaw, and through my teeth. I scream. I claw at my face, but hands pull my own down and away.

"It will pass. But it will return over and over so you must learn to master it." Valdis stares down at me. Is that pity I witness in his pale eyes?

I begin to shake. Whole full-body shudders that wrack my slight frame, perhaps I will rattle from my body and leave the shell of it behind. If only my mind could be free so easily. But it cannot. I have brokered a deal, and I must see it through.

A silver chain is dangled before me and, as the shudders abate, I resolve myself. What I have just endured will be nothing compared to what I am about to carry out.

"Go to your husband. Drop the contents of this vial into his drink, and when he is unconscious, chain both his wrists. I shall take care of the rest." The duke places a black vial and the silver chain into my trembling hands.

I look at him, trying to understand what kind of monster would do this to someone they were supposed to love. And then, as I clutch the items to me, it hits me like a wild wave… the same kind of monster as I now am.

I swallow, my throat coated with poisonous spikes. "Where will I find him?" I ask huskily.

"Allow me to escort you, dear daughter-in-law." The duke is all that is solicitous and proper now, as he holds out an arm. Repulsed, but with no other choice, I stand on legs that feel as though they will not hold me, and slip my arm through his. He smiles down at me, but it is Valdis I pay attention to. His face ripples with something like sympathy… something like regret, before he moves to open the door and allows the duke and I to leave.

As the duke and I traverse the tower steps and back to the main hallway, my senses are rioting. Everything seems brighter, sharper, somehow. Scents wash over me; the breeze from the narrow window carries with it the crisp snap of winter, and I pause, tilting my head up, while herby aromas snake up from deep below. My mouth waters as a different tang joins the others to tease my nostrils. In a disconcerting pull, my teeth lengthen.

"This is just the beginning," the duke murmurs, as horror ripples through me, warring with the seductive nature of all else.

I do not want this… I do not want this…

I lean against the stone wall, and the duke releases me. I want to take a deep breath, but there is no air for me. All I am is a creature created from blood and deceit, frozen in time; a twenty-year-old relic. My fingernails scratch against the stone beside me; the need to feel something real, something normal, is a bitter battle. A battle I shall never win again. But, the points on my teeth recede, and that is all I can call a win at this severed juncture in my existence.

"You are strong, my dear… let us see just how strong." The duke's tone holds a surprising amount of respect, and I allow him to once again take my arm and lead me the rest of the way along the hallway. We stop at a door, and the duke relinquishes his hold on me.

"My son awaits you. Remember, it is important *you* must be the one to entrap him, or the spell shall not hold." His bright blue gaze flashes, and I think of Nisette, of her future, and I nod in understanding.

Why the duke cannot carry out this vile plan himself, I know not. Why must he torture Nisette and I so? But I dare not question his motives. Not when Nisette's future hangs in the balance.

I place the silver chain in the pocket of my gown, and tuck the vial up into my long sleeve. I push open the door and the duke seems to melt away.

Lorcan turns from his position by the tall arched window. His hair is mussed as if he has been running his hands through it, while his cravat and jacket have been discarded. He stares at me for a long moment, then seeming to come to his senses, he rushes over to me.

"Rose, my love, I thought you were dead." He runs his hands over my face, to cup my chin, our eyes meeting in a clash of green and bright-blue.

I am dead.

But instead, I say, "I am fine, Lorcan. I do not remember what happened."

His eyes flash and he leads me over to a chair and settles me into it. "No recollection at all... of anything? Of why we are here?"

I am unsure how to answer. I want to tell him the truth, that I remember *everything*, that despite it all, for better or worse, he is my husband, and I am about to betray him in the most atrocious way imaginable. To curtail his freedom, deny him what his unnatural body will surely crave, prevent us from being together and sealing our union. I shake my head. Far better for him to believe I know not of this hidden dark life.

I cannot help myself though, and so I pull him down towards me, wanting to feel his lips on mine one final time. He obliges, even though I see the war in his eyes. He can see what I am, what I am becoming, but perhaps does not want to frighten me. Believing me ignorant. He shudders against my lips, and I let him in, sensing his surrender to the need coursing between us... back and forth like tiny currents. Tiny flickers, which could be teased into a raging storm if we let it.

I cannot let it.

I pull back. "Perhaps, some wine?" I ask, and, his eyes heavy with desire, he nods.

"Of course, my love." He turns away and as he pours out dark red wine from the carafe on the table into two heavy silver goblets, I slip the vial from my sleeve into my palm. Bitter, acrid daggers stab my tongue, and I arrange my face into a neutral expression as he turns back around holding the drinks.

He sets them down on the side table beside me, and I bide my time, every sinew snapping to attention.

"Rose, we must talk." He kneels before me, and goes to takes my hands. Panicked, I stand and grasp one goblet and turn my back on him, walking to the window. I hear him getting to his feet, so I quickly empty the vial into the goblet and slide the empty vessel back up my sleeve.

He joins me, just as I am swirling the goblet as if in thought. "Whatever it is, Lorcan, can it not wait?" I force a happy smile. "Surely, we should toast to finally being alone together first?"

A sad smile echoes on his face, and I know he is remembering our attempts at finding secluded areas at balls and often times being thwarted. I press my goblet into his hand and go and collect the second one.

"Very well," he says, but there is no happiness in his eyes as he murmurs, "to us." And raises his goblet. He must know what I know. That we are doomed. Our love is doomed. There can be no coming back from this. Though, he believes 'this' is something different, complex in its base form; a savage collision of worlds; light and dark. Not a wife condemning her husband.

But, did not he, by his wanton wish to be with me despite the separation of our natures, condemn me first?

No, I cannot put the blame wholly on him. I wanted him, *all* of him, from the moment of our meeting. I sensed there were hidden depths to him, and I longed to peel back his layers.

A shooting star arcs across the night sky, visible through the window. As Lorcan swallows deep, I think, *careful what you wish for...*

He blinks rapidly, and I set my own goblet down, un-drunk. I cannot toast to us, I do not have that privilege, for I have ensured there shall be no 'us'.

"Rose... what is happening?" Lorcan slurs and I go

to him. *I did what I had to, I am sorry, Lorcan… so sorry…* I help him to the bed, and his eyes are anguished on mine as he fights back the potion. He reaches out a hand.

I grasp it as tears stream down my face. I did not know I could still cry. I press his hand to mine. "Sleep, my love, sleep."

And he does.

I cannot prolong this agony, and so, I withdraw the silver chain and, as gently as I can, bind his wrists.

Nausea roils through me; acrid, acidic, and all-encompassing.

Blindly, I stumble from the room and I am caught in a firm embrace. "Well done, daughter. Now go and rest. Dawn approaches…"

Chapter
ELEVEN

"Hush." A soothing, husky voice awakens me and I realise I have been crying out in my sleep, as the past battered me ruthlessly.

I force open my eyes and see I am back in the present but the memory-cloaked-in-a-nightmare is still very much real. I am still at Castle Lamont, though one hundred years later.

But instead of Lirrel soothing me like the first night I awoke after my transformation, this time it is a blonde-haired female. She smiles gently, a hint of fangs showing behind her rosebud mouth. Her dark-blue eyes soften as they take me in.

"Who are you?" I ask.

"My name is Ines," she replies, and I feel no threat from her. She continues to dab my face with a soothing-scented cloth. "I am to care for you."

"Where is Mariette... Lorcan?" I ask, struggling to sit up.

Ines looks away for a moment, and dread curls

through me, fingers of it probing painfully. "I do not know where the young lady is," she admits, "but his lordship is in the connecting room to this one" — she meets my eyes — "he is unharmed."

Relief at that, at least, fills me. I do not understand what long charade Yves is playing, and what roles Lorcan and I are to play, but I know one thing. I shall no longer go meekly into the endless night, for a new emotion is unfurling within me like a black rose... each thorn on its dark stem dripping with one poisonous word... *revenge*. Revenge to the men who orchestrated my family's demise, who each rolled the dice and didn't care where they landed. Yves. Lirrel. My father-in-law and my former best friend. I will find a way to avenge my family, including—if I cannot save her now—Mariette... and to also free Lorcan. I do not yet know how I will accomplish any of it, but I do know that I need allies.

"My lady?"

I focus on Ines. "How long have you been here, Ines?" I ask her.

Her gaze turns haunted. "At Castle Lamont? One hundred years, but before that I was at Chateau LaCroix since my creation years before."

A hundred years. A century. All of us trapped. I had heard of Chateau LaCroix from Lirrel. It is the

European Court's stronghold in Paris. One of five seats. The others being in the Americas, The Russian Empire, Asia, and Britain. But the Paris and London courts are closely entwined.

"If you don't mind my asking, why did you leave the chateau?" I ask gently, knowing the boundaries so tightly guarded by some could fracture into terrifying flashbacks.

"The duke had need for my unique skills, and so I was brought here." Ines toys with the cloth, before setting it back into the bowl on the table beside the bed I am lying on.

"Unique skills?" I ask, suddenly feeling the bed turn to water as I unsteadily try to grasp my shifting thoughts.

She stares at me, her eyes darkening somewhat. "Indeed. Before I was turned I was a healer—some would say, witch, but I prefer healer now. I stayed back your initial death, my lady, however briefly. I am not sorry for that, but I am sorry for what happened to you afterwards. I was brought here to assist Valdis, and the duke commands us to do his bidding."

I cannot blame her. How can I? We have all been forced to do things that we never wanted to be a part of. "It is all right, Ines," I tell her and her face clears. "But why are you still here? Are you privy to further plans?"

She shrugs delicately. "I was to remain here for one hundred years. I know not of what the duke plans next, except that we leave for Paris in the evening. All of us."

"All?" I ask, surprised. *What* is Yves planning?

"Indeed, New Year's Eve is in mere days. It is Duc LaCroix's turn to host the centennial ball."

A new century. A new era. I cannot believe I am still here to see it. But at what cost? I need to think. I need to speak with Lorcan.

Ines leans forward and takes one of my hands, her voice lowering to a whisper. "I know you do not want this life... I can help you. I assisted Valdis in creating the potion that sustained you. I have something similar. It replaces the body's need for..." she trails off and I know what she refers to. How can I not? "Just one drop daily and you can survive, survive and not partake."

I cannot believe what she is offering. "Why help me?"

"Because I do not wish this life either and I know what it is to have to fight back the urges. It is monstrous, and excruciating, and if I can ease another's suffering then I will do everything in my power. They shall not win." Her face becomes animated and I see not only an ally, but perhaps, a friend.

"I appreciate your offer more than I can convey,

Ines, but how shall I avoid the duke forcing me to drink?" I am feeling hopeful for the first time since I was changed.

"He does not know the complexity of the spell Valdis and I created. You can delay him for a while longer. Show him how strong you are, show him that you are still able to function despite it. That you can fight the urges, and still survive."

"But will Valdis tell him?" I am all too aware of putting one's trust in the wrong person. I had learned it in such a devastating manner. I hope I am not making another mistake by putting my trust in Ines, but I can see no reason why she would wish to trick me.

"Valdis does not know what I work on in secret… but he is not as awful as you might think. He has been good to me. I trust him." Ines smiles sadly.

But that did not mean *I* should trust him. My trust would not be offered lightly again, and so, I would take up Ines's offer, but still keep my wits about me. I will surely need them. Especially if we are to travel to Paris, and into an unknown court and all its inside politics and machinations.

"Then, thank you, Ines. I would be glad of a friend. If I can do anything to help you in return, please let me know."

She regards me steadily for a moment, then nods.

"Your friendship will be enough for now, my lady."

"Roselle, please." I smile at her and she smiles back. I look at the connecting door. "I must go to my husband now."

"Of course, I will see you this evening. I will get your doses ready." Ines stands, smooths down her gown of dark-blue silk, and inclines her head. "Goodbye for now, Roselle."

"Goodbye, Ines, and thank you."

My new friend leaves my chamber, and I lie against the pillows for one long moment. Taking in everything that has occurred, every deceit, every revelation, every fractured moment and try to piece them back together to create a picture I can make sense of. I let my new resolve settle in my bones.

But first I need to confess to Lorcan. I cannot continue to hold the weight of my guilt above us, like a guillotine, ready to drop at any moment and sever our bond. It is already tenuous, frayed. I needed to find a way to stitch it back together.

Determined now, I swing my legs off the bed and walk over to the connecting door. Distractedly, I note I wear a long, diaphanous nightgown of almost sheer black organza and lace, tied at the neck with a satin black bow. My bare feet make no sound on the thick carpet. I tap the connecting door and at Lorcan's gruff,

"Come in," I turn the handle and push open the door.

Lorcan reclines on his bed, garbed only in black trousers. "Hello, love, I hope you have recovered from your ordeal," he says as I hesitate. A shadow cuts across his face and I cannot read his expression, but his tone is husky and sated. I am suddenly unsure of this version of him. I have known many versions of the man I now call husband. Society gentleman, terrified protector, loving despite the years passed, and now this one, who appears ready to finally claim me.

"Lorcan, I—" I begin, knowing it will be far better to say it all now, air the wound before it festers. To speak of what occurred after I broke down following the revelation of Lirrel's long betrayal. How we are still unharmed and allowed to be with each other... and at last, tell him the truth of our separation.

"Come here," Lorcan interrupts me, sitting up and finally, I see his eyes. Heavy yet intense. Compelling.

I cannot *be* compelled by him, but I still feel as though I am. Without realising it, I am floating across the room towards him, *my husband*, my blood suddenly thrumming, not with the need of the thirst but with a wholly intrinsic need. One of the flesh.

"Lorcan..."

"Hush, love," he says, "let me help you heal," and his mouth is on mine. Devouring, claiming, searing.

Teeth scraping, kiss deepening until we are as one. Fused together as though our combined heat has melted the seams of us. My hands trails over his chest, tracing the hard contours of his muscles, still starker than they should be, but strangely honed as though no time at all has passed for him.

Perhaps, he has supped until rejuvenated. The thought gives me pause, and I pull back, but he unties the bow of my nightgown and lowers his head, and all rational thought scatters.

He trails hot kisses along my collarbone, one for every year we were apart, until I cannot bear it. I hate myself, but cannot stop myself. Whatever is happening between us has taken on a life of its own. It breathes where we do not. Binds that which is broken. For one still, time-frozen moment, we will have this. Have each other.

"Rose," Lorcan murmurs against my skin, "may I finally seal our union?"

"*Yes*," I declare. He raises his head, disconcerting me by the sudden predatory look there, but it is instantly replaced by a look so fiercely loving that I dismiss it. I know what he is. What I am. Of course it will force its way through. The beast lurks a mere thin layer beneath the surface, no matter how hard we try to keep it at bay.

A low growl in his throat, Lorcan dispenses of our clothes and ranges himself over me. And whatever is left of my soul whispers, "*finally.*"

I am fire and ice combined. Heat pools low in my stomach while tiny crystalline fragments of frost freeze my limbs, immobilising me. I do not wish to move; I only wish to savour the exquisite feel of Lorcan claiming my body. Claiming it in the only way I ever wish to be claimed. By him. Only by him. The fire wins, and suddenly it is pooling outwards, like an inferno roaring through me until I am moving, moving beneath him to his rhythm. His dance. There is no pain, only a tension that melts away in the face of the flames flickering between us.

I never want this to end because I know what follows. Now that I know him this way, I will mourn his inevitable loss in a keener, deeper, way. For how will he ever want to touch me again after I reveal all?

But it ends, as all delight inevitably must. Still I cling to him, my legs and arms wrapped around him, delaying what is now unavoidable. He kisses my hair, lingering, as if he himself is delaying something.

He pulls from my hold, and I let go, feeling cold, suddenly, so very cold. The ice making its way back through the cracks of my stilled heart.

Lorcan stares down at me. "I have waited one

hundred years for this," he whispers, a catch in his voice.

Oh, darkness, what have I done?

Tears gather in my eyes. I find my voice. "I must tell you," I say and his whole face changes, and I blink and he is gone from me. He stands near the curtained windows, bathed in shadows.

"Do not speak of it, Rose, for I know. I *know*." His voice is anguished, tortured. And in this moment I become horribly aware that he already knows of my betrayal. He knew before I even came to him. Before he just sealed our union. The duke has already revealed it to him. Oh, how he must be laughing now. He waited one hundred years for this very moment. For the knife to cut the deepest. He has won. He has proven to Lorcan that choosing me was folly, that I would betray him. *Had* betrayed him. Yves had devised this whole century-long travesty, serving up the final act when it would be the most impactful.

"Lorcan, *please*, let me explain…"

But Lorcan has already gathered up his clothes and is at the door. "There is nothing to explain, Wife," he utters in a dead voice, and is gone.

I lie in my own shame, thick and cloying, and though I knew I would feel wretched after the reveal, I am not prepared for the depth of it. I cannot move, can no longer think in coherent sentences.

Instead, I close my eyes, allowing the tears to run unchecked down my face to pool in the hollow of my throat. Perhaps they will overflow and I will drown in them. What a farcical notion. There can be no easy release for me. Not until I have taken my revenge. Now Yves deserves it more than ever. For not giving me the chance to explain to Lorcan.

Perhaps Lorcan would have understood that I had *no* choice in what I did, but I should have seized my chance when I had been given it at George's farmhouse. What a coward I am. What a fool.

But, whatever happens, I will find a way to avenge all the wrongs Duke Lamont has wrought.

He is powerful, but I am fury itself.

If a monster he has created, then a monster I will become, but with only two targets in mind.

I tuck my grief away. Lock it deep within me, as far down as it possibly will go. It will be my fuel, the tinder to the firestorm I shall unleash.

And so, we will go to Paris, and I will play my part.

I hope the duke is ready for the adversary he has unwittingly created. I hope Lirrel is prepared for me to pay him back in kind for his 'loyalty'.

In the darkness, I smile. Slow and thoughtful.

I have always wanted to go to Paris.

Perhaps, it will be all I ever dreamed it would be... but with the added satisfaction of a family avenged... a century of wrongs righted... and, hopefully, wistfully, a love re-found.

I have much to do. Much to plan for.

I only wish Lorcan was by my side.

I run a hand across the sheets beside me, before turning over and curling into a ball. I allow myself the indulgence of a moment of sorrow and solitude.

Then, *then*, I shall rise and prepare.

Chapter TWELVE

The ship rocks beneath my booted feet. I adjust the hood of my black velvet cloak and try to drown out the raucous sounds around me.

I have not seen Lorcan, Lirrel or even the duke. Ines collected me from my rooms, and escorted me into a carriage, along with a silent and brooding guard; his presence making it impossible to speak freely, but Ines managed to pass me a vial discreetly. Together, we travelled the few hours to the coast, boarding the large vessel before dawn kissed the horizon.

Now, I stand alone, feet planted, hand gripping the railing as the coast of France comes into view. We spent the daylight hours out on the channel, only coming close to the coast as the moon shrugged off its shroud and revealed its full, shining face. I am grateful to be lost in my own little world. The sounds around me from Yves' crew and court fade away as I dream and plot.

My first undertaking is to reconcile with Lorcan. I

believed I was strong enough to let him go, that my sins precluded me from finding redemption with him. If only I could explain *why* I had done what I did. If we could discuss both of our failings, then perhaps, perhaps, we could find a way to forgive each other. But, I fear, it will be no easy task. I can still recall his face when he left me in his chamber after we finally became husband and wife in truth. Devastation twinned with anger. But still, he made our union official despite knowing. That alone gave me hope.

One loose black curl trails against my cheek as a gentle breeze guides us into the port at Le Havre. I note a line of black carriages await our disembarkment.

"Ah, Roselle, there you are, my dear. You shall travel with me and Lorcan. We must put on a united front, mustn't we?" Yves joins me at the railing, his eyes on the activity on the dockside.

Thankful of the dose I had taken as soon as I was able, I can pull from its strength, and turn demurely to the duke. "Of course, Your Grace."

His eyes narrow briefly, the only sign of his surprise at my apparent acquiescence to him. At the demure personage I present—a stark contrast to the screaming, wailing one he saw of me last. "I trust you shall behave as befits your new status? Lirrel will be joining us in a few days. I thought perhaps it would be prudent to allow you some time to deal with your emotions." He says *emotions* as if it is an affliction of the weak.

But I am not weak. I have never felt stronger.

I stare at him steadily, all while the anger flickers softly inside me. It is strange how easy it is to bank it, to not allow it to take free rein. But, I am no stranger to biding my time. This shall be no different. One hundred years of torment. One hundred years of jagged memories. I can endure a few more days. If Lorcan and I cannot reconcile, then I shall bow out gracefully. I lower my head.

But I will not go alone.

Lirrel, at least, shall be accompanying me. He wanted to spend eternity with me—my lips curve into a smile, unseen by Yves—then, I shall happily oblige.

I raise my chin and speak. "I have quite recovered," I tell him, and he regards me for a long time, but I offer a small smile, and he finally nods.

"Very good, my dear. I would hate to have to re-think yours and Lorcan's positions within my court," Yves says in an approving, yet tinged with warning, tone. "I see now why my son chose you—not merely for your beauty—which I admit is quite remarkable, especially in this form, but for your inner strength... you need to be strong," he adds almost to himself.

What is beauty? I ponder. A mask, a surface façade. The equivalent of a siren's lure, drawing you in close… closer… closer still… until it is too late to see the monster beneath. This time, I let out a full smile, allowing my fangs to reveal themselves. "Thank you," I say, and I am surprised to see the duke appear flustered. Good. I can use that to my advantage. I do not yet know what he plans for Lorcan and I, but for now, he seems content to allow us a place by his side as we enter the European Court's new year celebrations. What is that saying? *Keep your friends close, but your enemies closer*? I shall resolve to do just that and play the dutiful daughter-in-law to exquisite precision.

"Your Grace, we are ready to disembark." Adair joins us, his eyes flicking to me, but I settle my face into a neutral expression, before turning away and resuming my perusal of the dockside.

"Excellent. Where is my son?" Yves asks.

Adair pauses, then, "He is finishing up his meal."

I stiffen. I cannot help it. I know what he is, what his body so obviously hungers for, but still it cuts me to the quick. This sickening knowledge of what my husband carries out in the dark. When shadows coat him, and the red film blankets his mind, and he forsakes all reason. When the craving takes a hold, and whispers seductively against his skin in hot flaming licks. I know it. I have endured it. I will, continue, to endure it.

"Roselle, be a dear, and go and collect your husband."

I startle at the words. My tongue darts out to run along my lips, whether in nervousness or to prevent myself from a quick denial I know not. I can imagine what he does to stay alive, but I have no wish to see it. Ever.

I stare from a now darkly-amused Adair to the duke. At the cruel delight displayed in his blue eyes. I steel myself. He is testing me. Again. Will there be no end to his twisted games? Of course not. Who am I fooling?

I straighten. "Where might I find him?" I ask softly, and take a brief moment to savour the instant Adair's face changes comically fast.

Yves, however, does not react. Perhaps we are equally matched. He moves, I counter-move. Like a dance. But still I feel like a marionette, and he holds my strings. Instead, he says, "He is in the cabin next to yours. I am surprised you had not discovered that fact for yourself. I know what newlyweds are like."

Bile rises in my throat at the mocking tone. We have not been newlyweds for one hundred years. "Indeed," I say neutrally, and dip a quick curtsy, before

I turn—my long mauve dress swishing along the deck—and head down the wooden steps leading to the cabins in the bowels of the large ship.

I keep my head down, and make no eye contact with any of the compelled crew readying the ship for disembarking. I carry on until I get to three cabins at the end of the corridor. I discount the door with the duke's crest on, deducing it to be Yves' cabin, and instead knock the door the other side of the one I had rested in alone. Sleep had eluded me. Instead, I had stayed in a kind of stasis, held in place by the rocking of the boat; it's momentum like a pendulum. Back and forth. Back and forth, like a clock ticking down the seconds to my demise.

I knock again when my first knock goes unanswered. This time, I hear muffled sounds, and dread curling deep within me, I am transported back to the garden the first time I had met Lorcan, when mewling, whimpering sounds came from within the hedge maze…

You do not want to go in there…

No, I did not, but this time, I must.

I push open the door, and stop short, the dread curdling into abject horror. Sights, sounds, scents, coalesce, fracture, and then reassemble to create a picture so abhorrent, so unthinkable that I almost do not believe what I am actually seeing.

Mariette. Sweet Mariette.

"No. Lorcan… *no*," I moan, the volume almost indecipherable, but still he hears. He spins to me, lowering Mariette to the bed, his face a picture of shock. I feel as though I am witnessing the scene from a great height, while the version of me that is clinging to the doorframe is no longer me, but a broken statue hewn from horror, and tacked together with veins made of severed trust.

"Roselle… what…?" Lorcan shakes his head as if words are foreign to him.

Mariette is deathly white, the two puncture wounds on her neck stand out starkly like two red full stops. The end. The end of all she knew, the end of the future she was to have. I cannot move, my fingers have fused themselves to the door frame, while my boots can barely hold up my leaden legs. I cannot stop staring at her, willing her to return.

Ines!

The thought of my new friend, has hope pooling into me, spearing outwards to unfasten my fingers and reanimate my legs.

I do not spare Lorcan a glance, not even when he seems to come around from his own torpor and aim for me, one hand outstretched, his eyes earnest.

I rush away with Lorcan calling desperately after me. Now it is I who run from him. Betrayal after betrayal we heap upon each other. When will it peak? When the mound has become so vast that neither of us can breach it? Until it smothers us beneath its weight.

The duke is right. How many times can my stilled heart break before *I* break? No, I refuse to break before it is done. Then, I shall not care how many pieces I shatter into, whether my heart crumbles into dust and scatters to the winds. Because then the fracturing will have meaning. I grasp at meaning, because without it, what am I?

I grip my skirts and run along the corridor. I tap on the door I know to be Ines' cabin, frantically hoping she is still inside. "Ines? Ines, I need you," I say against the wooden panels.

The door is pulled open and I almost fall forward. Ines ushers me inside her room, her dark blue eyes wide as she takes in my stricken state. She closes the door and leans against it. "What is it? We are about to leave."

"I need your help. It is Mariette, she is…" I cannot say the words, so I swallow and try again. "… she is dying. Can you help her as you did me, all those years ago?"

Pity ripples across her face. "We cannot risk

getting caught. The duke cannot know I am assisting *you*, let alone a mortal girl."

"Please, Ines. It is my fault she is caught up in all this. *Please.*" I am fully ready to beg on my knees.

And all my fault that Lorcan spiralled into such a pit of misery that he chose the path that led to darkness and death. But I cannot think on that. Time, like Mariette's life force, is slipping away.

Ines pushes away from the door and, seemingly coming to a decision, picks up a small velvet bag from next to a larger bag set on her narrow bed, and says, "Very well, but just this one time only. Getting her to safety will be up to you."

Relief floods me. "Thank you, Ines, thank you," I say then we hurry from her room.

I have no notion of what will await us back in Lorcan's cabin, but seeing him staunching her wounds with a muslin cloth is not what I expect. Ines and I exchange a swift look before she moves to take over from him.

I hover, unsure what to do with myself, but my eyes are riveted on Mariette, and Ines' ministrations. I sense Lorcan move around the bed and stand near me, and feel the weight of his gaze on the side of my face; but it is the scent of his shame that affects me the most.

... I was the one who found her after her attack... a line

was crossed that night… Suffice it to say I was punished
when I returned from taking her to safety…

The words overwhelm me, as if Lorcan himself repeats them to me, and not simply dredged up from the memory of what he revealed to me about Coralie at George and Marta's farmhouse. My disgust of him falters—*but my self-disgust remains*. I cannot reconcile how *that* man, a man who went out of his way, at great cost to his own safety, could then attack another innocent young girl. It does not feel right. Something is off. I suddenly do not believe he is capable of such an about-turn. Surely, he is stronger than that. Surely, he would not blame Mariette for *my* failings.

Now, I do look at him. Truly look at him. I note the bloodshot eyes, the tremor of his hands, the sheen on his pallid face. The anguish written clearly upon it.

"He was drugged," Ines says softly, and I pull my gaze away to meet hers as she straightens away from Mariette's prone figure, and gestures at a goblet on the side table. I wince as the past comes back to haunt me— *taunt* me—once again. "He never hurt Mariette. This is Elize's work, I can smell her all over the girl. I suspect Mariette was attacked and then left here for Lord Lorcan to finish off."

Lorcan slumps in obvious relief. At this revelation, I am suddenly unsure of myself. Of us.

Ines speaks softly, interrupting the now painful eye contact between Lorcan and I. "She will heal. I caught her just in time. The potion I gave her will stimulate blood reproduction, but it will take a day or two. You must protect her, then see her safely away."

Lorcan says, "I have friends in Paris. I will ensure her safe passage back to England."

I ask softly, "How will we ensure that she remains safe until that time?" It isn't that I do not trust him, but more a genuine worry that Elize, Adair, and the duke will not relinquish their toy, and subsequently their hold over me, so easily.

"Let me handle that." I stare at him, and he makes a noise of frustration. "Roselle, I know trust is an issue between us, but you *must* trust me. I promise she will be safe."

Trust him? How can I fully trust him when I cannot even trust myself to not make another rash decision in the name of love? But, as a terse knock comes on the door, I have no choice *but* to put my trust in him.

Ines, to my surprise, seems to blend into the wall, and I blink at the spot where she had stood. A healer, she had told me, but her talents seem to go beyond that. I have no time to further my thoughts on the matter as Lorcan goes and wrenches open the door.

"The duke requires your presence," I hear Draven say, and I flinch, knowing I failed the test in collecting my husband myself.

"We shall join him in a moment," Lorcan replies, and closes the door firmly, before leaning on it, and running a hand through his hair.

Ines rematerialises and casts me a look. "I have learned how to blend seamlessly into the background," she explains.

"No doubt a shrewd skill," I acknowledge, thinking of how I would like to slip unnoticed through this narrow dark strip of the world I now inhabit. But vanishing is not an avenue open to me presently. The duke will no doubt ensure mine and Lorcan's humiliation will be front and centre when he so chooses.

"Shrewd, indeed," Ines murmurs back. "I should be going. I will see you soon."

I place a hand on her arm as she moves past me. "Thank you, Ines. I am in your debt once again."

"No debt," she says, but yet I hope to be able to help her if I can. She curtsies quickly at Lorcan before he moves away from the door and allows her to slip out into the corridor.

Save for the still slumbering Mariette, I am now alone with my husband.

We stare at each other for one long moment.

"Lorcan, there is much to talk of." He regards me steadily, and I take heart that he does not cut me off. "Perhaps, we can find a moment later?"

His eyes rove over me, and I resist the urge to twist my hands together. After a moment, he gives a jerky nod, and relief floods me.

He moves over to Mariette and lifts her, settling her over his shoulder. I do not know what his plan is, but when he turns to me, his eyes are now clear, and determined.

"Trust me," he repeats and moves to the open door.

I follow, trepidation dogging my hasty steps.

Chapter THIRTEEN

"What is all this?"

Elize's voice takes on one of baffled amusement.

In a voice I do not recognise, Lorcan says, as he deposits Mariette inside the carriage, "Food for the journey, of course."

I school my face into an impassive mask when Elize flicks a delighted look my way as I wait next to the duke's carriage on the dockside. "I do hope you will share?" She licks her lips as if she hadn't already stolen more than a taste of Mariette already. For one heady moment I see myself slapping her face until her cheeks resemble the colour of her blood-red lips.

"*Mine*," Lorcan growls, and I am gratified that Elize actually flinches.

"Well, no need to be so territorial, Lorcan, it is most vulgar," she snaps, before shooting me another look, this time one of indignation. She turns on her heel and stalks off to the carriage behind the duke's. *Good riddance.*

"Indeed, Son, most vulgar, but in this instance, I will allow it. I am happy to see you are partaking fully once again. Your long abstinence obviously worked wonders in changing your mind." Yves melts out of the shadows and I stay the shudder that hovers over my skin, like ghostly fingertips indelibly raising each hair on my arms, without even touching me.

Lorcan dips his head, but his shoulders tense briefly and my hand almost inches out to soothe the tension away. But I do not have that right. Not when I am the cause of it. "You have got what you wanted," he replies, and the duke lets out a low laugh.

"Almost, my son, almost," Yves says. He barely spares me a look before he holds out his hand.

I take it, and step up into the carriage to settle myself next to the still Mariette, but feel woefully inadequate to fight the duke if he should pounce. Lorcan joins us and sits opposite Mariette, while the duke faces me. The door closes and entombs us. The black interior of the carriage is stifling and with no sounds, save for the gentle hush of air escaping from Mariette, I can almost believe this is where I shall spend eternity. The thought of my revenge shall be all that gets me through this long torturous journey.

Trust me…

The carriage sets off with a jolt, and the silence

becomes almost unbearable. But I know Yves is perfectly poised, watching my every movement, my every expression, so I remain still and poised myself, recalling every deportment and etiquette lesson. Oh, how proud Mama would be if she could see how straight my back is, how my head is tilted at just the right angle, how a small moue graces my lips, how my hands are folded just so. All that is needed is a vapid expression, and my empty-headed-debutante look would be complete. The foolish thought almost causes a hysterical laugh to burst from me. But I know better. Oh, I know better than to betray anything.

"You do not know how pleased I am to learn you have finally consummated your marriage. It must have been a terrible trial for you... with only Lirrel for *company*, my dear."

Now who is being vulgar? Distaste, heavy and malignant, coats my tongue at his insinuation, making it hard to form a reply. Lorcan does not even twitch at his father's obvious attempt at baiting him. Baiting me. But then, Lorcan has been playing his father's games for far, far longer than I. I wonder just how long.

"I am more than pleased to be reunited with my husband," I reply, refusing to acknowledge mention of Lirrel.

"And is he—ah—*pleased* to be reunited with *you*?"

A sliver of moonlight slants in through the carriage window and highlights Yves' eyes. They dance merrily. Oh, how he enjoys this swordfight. Parry and thrust. Sidestep and lunge. But my sword is just as sharp, honed through years of torment.

"It certainly appeared so." I allow a hint of satisfaction to curl into my words. Evoking a sense of a long night of desire between two who had been denied each other's pleasure for too long. I lean back, and allow one hand to trail up to my neck, as though sated at just the mere memory of our reunion.

Lorcan looks across at me, while the duke frowns. "Touché, my dear," he murmurs, while a sudden languid grin slides onto my husband's face.

"Indeed, Father. I am more than pleased," Lorcan says, his eyes holding my gaze.

Careful, I want to say even while delicious sensation roves up and down inside me; a purr of satiation, *do not reveal too much, even if you are merely playing the part of the besotted husband*. For how could he sincerely be pleased? We are yet to reconcile in truth, though the body had been more than willing to fuse the bond back together.

A languid smile of his own graces Yves' face, and he leans forward, one sharp-nailed hand brushing the skirts of my gown. "As well you should be pleased, my son, your bride is a jewel." Though he spoke to Lorcan, his intense eyes feast on me. "Have a care that she is not... stolen from you. Thieves abound within both our court and at Chateau LaCroix."

I hiss back my retort, but Lorcan has no such compunction. "I will kill any who even dares lays one finger upon her," he says in low, even tones, and my mouth parts in surprise as I stare at my husband.

A deep, dark laugh fills the carriage, breaking my staring gaze.

"How *splendid* to have you back, Son." Yves appears delighted. He nods. "Yes, keeping your wife was a sage notion indeed." And my still heart yearns to thunder in fear. Lorcan has thrown caution to the wind, and revealed the depth of his feeling. Though perhaps, it is not through love he reacts, he has nevertheless staked a claim on me, one that has proven that I am his weakness. *And he, is mine.*

I stare at him once again, trying desperately to understand him. Understand why he would reveal so much. To our enemy no less.

Lorcan rises his chin—the absence of fear clear in his gaze—and I can only hope that he knows what he is doing.

For I know what the duke is truly capable of, and son or not, he will do whatever he deems necessary for the survival of his court.

"Now," Yves regards us both. "Enough of the frivolity. As I said before, we must display a united front. Nothing less will be tolerated." He looks solely at me. "Even when Lirrel joins us, you shall act with decorum as befits your status. Do I make myself clear?"

Fully aware of the slumbering Mariette beside me, I school my features into an impassive mask, and incline my head. "I understand," I tell him demurely. Though my hands clasp, claw-like, in the folds of my gown, that is the only bodily release I allow of my true feelings rioting within me.

Do not show weakness, emit no fear.

Even though the beast within longs to tear Lirrel apart limb from limb and scatter his ashes far and wide. Erasing his being and the very essence of him from the world that he dared sully with his rotten duplicity.

Yves nods in approval at me and my eyes slide away, only to be captured by Lorcan's astute gaze. He knows, I think. He knows my true feelings. Despite the passing of time, he can still read me as if what is etched on my soul is laid bare before him, to be transcribed by his eyes alone. I only hope he does not prevent me from doing what *I* must do.

Only then can the debt be paid. The one, that not only Lirrel owes, but I owe too.

His betrayal is no less than my own, but I seek redemption of a different kind. One that can only be granted by the man sat across from me. The man, who, in another life, would have been my husband before the eyes of God, and not the dark deity that claimed us instead.

I allow a glimmer of that truth to infuse my gaze, gifting Lorcan with the promise that Lirrel will indeed pay. If I do nothing else, Lirrel *will* pay.

I can but hope my husband believes my only motive is because of what his cousin did to my family, and not that he considers me nothing but a scorned lover who spent a century with a man who had orchestrated his own way of luring her there. That is something I will endeavour to convince my love of. Darkness only knows that if the roles had been reversed and Lorcan had spent lifetimes alone with another, my heart would have shattered in two beneath the weight of doubt. I regard him thoughtfully. Does he too seek revenge?

Perhaps, our wants will converge. A fusion of so many layers of reprisals. I intend to gift him with that too. Lirrel has not only wronged me, but Lorcan too. Shame licks at me. Shame that I allowed Lirrel to create an illusion of an existence and mock what I should have shared with Lorcan. What was *stolen* from Lorcan.

The duke is right; thieves abound.

But this time *I* will be the thief. Stealthy in my pursuit of the ultimate heist. One that would steal the very being of Lirrel. So that not even a fragment of him remains.

This is my promise.

This is my gift to my husband.

I release a smile as the carriage judders to a halt, and awareness steals into Lorcan's eyes.

"Come, my children. We have arrived." The duke smiles around at us, and I instinctively settle a hand on Mariette's wrist, an action that does not go unnoticed by him. His smile turns indulgent. "You may keep your toy… but take care. There are those here, who believe in sharing." He turns his gaze on Lorcan, and his smile morphs into one of savagery.

Lorcan does not break eye contact, instead it is the duke who concedes as the carriage door is opened and Adair frames the doorway.

It is a small win, but a win nonetheless.

The duke alights, followed by Lorcan, who holds out a hand to me. I gently rouse Mariette and her eyelids flutter. She opens her gaze and though I hate it, I look to Lorcan. With a sigh, he drops his hand and instead leans back into the carriage and looks deep into Mariette's eyes. I see the panic building and he quickly assuages it. "You are safe, come," he says in a hypnotic tone.

I feel as though it is I who needs rousing from whatever spell Lorcan is wreaking, but I know his effect on me is because of an entirely different compulsion. One I weave all on my own.

Mariette does not hesitate. She rises and allows Lorcan to lead her from the carriage and I swiftly follow. Intent on being her shadowy protector.

Lorcan, Mariette and I stand close together while the duke confers with Adair. The other black carriages pull up behind us and I get my first look at Chateau LaCroix.

Where Castle Lamont is dark and brooding, a hovering, waiting tomb, Duc LaCroix's seat is a silvery-grey shadow wrought from a multitude of towers and wings held up with gleaming marble pillars. No gargoyles leer down from the crenelated roof, instead winged angels poise in mid-flight, or perhaps readying to fall. Fall all the way from heaven's glory to the mortal plane and claim their position among the ranks of the darkly depraved.

But do they not know that what they already hold within their pearly palms far surpasses what can be found here? This is no pleasure garden, merely the gateway to hades. I should know. The moment I died, and was reborn—on the very same plane—solidified the understanding that we make our own hell. Each and every one of us.

I turn my head, inadvertently catching Lorcan's eye, and a chink of light illuminates my stone-entombed heart. Perhaps, a glimpse of heaven can be found even in the deepest of hells. After all, Lucifer was an angel once.

With the duke still distracted, it affords me a moment to voice my concerns. "What of Mariette. How will you ensure her safety?" I whisper, and Lorcan shoots me a warning look. Even whispers can be discerned as a shout for those with the capability of hearing it.

"Leave all with me," Lorcan replies, his voice no louder than a sigh breathed fathoms away.

I have no choice but to trust him.

The duke turns from Adair, and his eyes flicker. Silently, one by one the other carriage doors open and Adair strides forward to knock the silver knocker of the chateau. I place a hand to my brow at the dizzying spectral dance orchestrated by a mere eye flicker. Power exudes in an almost visual aura encompassing the duke, perhaps emphasized by two courts converging. My resolve falters at the notion. How will I ever compete with such ancient forces combined?

I find my hand gripped briefly, and I look down to see Lorcan's hand retreating stealthily away from mine. I meet his eyes and the look I see there restores me. Fortifies me.

Despite our tenuous relationship, I am no longer alone.

Ines glides serenely alongside Valdis to join the duke and she glances my way.

No, I am no longer alone.

Even after the longest and hottest of days, the moon always arises to soothe the scorched ground with its healing light. A balm for those in need.

I allow the knowledge of my no longer solitary path to succour me.

As the door to Chateau LaCroix is opened and an impossibly tall, supernaturally handsome dark-brown haired man advances from within, I ready myself to face whatever comes next in this path of redemption.

Chapter FOURTEEN

"My dear Yves, you have arrived."

"Valentin, Cousin, a pleasure to see you again. It has been far too long." Duke Lamont clasps the outstretched hand of the man.

"What is one hundred years to old friends and family?"

I tense at the words, acutely aware of Lorcan by my side. Would he think such a notion?

Yves smiles widely. "Indeed." He turns to Lorcan and I, a mocking light in his eyes. "You remember my son, Lorcan, of course, but we have since been blessed with a new addition to our family. Roselle, come here." His tone, though silken, hides a steel edge.

I paste a smile on my face, one I would have worn at a Society ball when being introduced to a member of the upper echelons, and walk forward to accept Yves' outstretched hand. He pulls me close to his side.

"This is my son's new bride, Lady Roselle. Roselle, this is my cousin and the head of the European Court,

Duc Valentin LaCroix."

I am hardly a new bride, but I let the misleading statement flitter away and instead give my most gracious curtsy to the duc.

One long finger beneath my chin arises me, and I meet Valentin LaCroix's piercing blue eyes. "*Enchantée*, my dear." He looks beyond me. "You are very lucky in securing such a beauty, Lorcan."

"She is more than simply beauty," Lorcan replies in an even tone, and Valentin lets out a wide smile, and impales me once again with his gaze.

"Let us hope so," he says enigmatically. He releases me from his observation, and I understand that the power Yves holds is frail by comparison. I will need to be careful here. So very careful.

The duc raises his voice. "Welcome Court Lamont, you are all invited inside." He sweeps one arm wide in a grand gesture, before leading us all into the expansive foyer of the chateau.

I stay close to Lorcan and, in turn, to a hazy-eyed Mariette. I only hope we shall be shown to our chambers with haste, as many curious eyes devour us from the doorways of numerous rooms and from those waiting on the curved marble staircase dominating the centre of the foyer. One vast crystal chandelier hangs from the domed ceiling and illuminates the area in sharp, glittering daggers of light.

Elize comes up on my other side. "You have not seen opulence until you have experienced a ball at Chateau LaCroix," she remarks haughtily.

I am surprised she seeks me out for conversation after the scene at the carriage. "I look forward to it," I say, and she tosses me a knowing smirk.

I watch as the smile seems to freeze on her face, and I follow her gaze. A woman has joined Duc LaCroix. She is ethereally beautiful with dainty features enhanced by her immortality. Her amber eyes seem to glow, while her deep auburn hair curls around her delicate cheekbones in glossy waves. She wears a gown of muted bronze that complements her pale skin, seemingly suffusing it with warmth.

"Katerin. What is she doing here?" Elize mutters, her lips twisting.

Surprised at seeing the usually poised Lady Sorrence so tense, I turn to look at her, but my attention is captured by Adair who joins his wife. An astonished look crosses his face as he sees the woman, before he pulls his gaze away. Elize gives him a pointed glare, and his jaw firms.

Interesting.

I do not have time to prolong my thoughts about what kind of history the trio have, as the duc claps his hands and compelled servants move through the crowd. "You shall be taken to your rooms now, and I urge you all to rest. For tonight the revelry begins."

Those from Court Lamont follow the servants up the sweeping staircase, and I place myself strategically so Mariette is sandwiched between Lorcan and I as we ascend. Nostrils flare and eyes turn her way as we pass by.

I throw Lorcan a look over her head. We must get Mariette out of here promptly. *She is not safe.*

His returned gaze reiterates his earlier statement. *Trust me.*

I am in a strange place, with even stranger companions. I *must* put my faith in my husband.

As we turn at the top of the stairs towards the left tower, I look over the balcony and notice Ines speaking closely with the duc in the foyer where he stands with Katerin, and I recall her telling me she once belonged to his court. The duc looks up, catching me looking, and instinctively I drop my gaze. A fleeting fear runs through me. Though I felt no hesitation in trusting Ines, her loyalties no doubt lie with Duc LaCroix. I hope my new friend will not betray me in any way.

"Come now, Roselle. Do not linger. I am sure you wish to sequester yourself with your husband." Duke Lamont passes me with a vulgar smirk.

I cannot help the flush that stains my cheeks as Lorcan looks back to see what is keeping me. I hasten my steps and join him as a servant stops at a door.

"My lord, my lady, these are your rooms," the servant intones and opens the door on the right, then indicates the door further along the corridor. "They have a connecting door." He bows then carries on his slow, almost puppet-like way.

Mine and Lorcan's eyes meet in a heated clash, before Lorcan breaks the gaze and opens the door.

"For protection's sake, we must stay close," Lorcan says gruffly.

"Of course," I say, "for protection's sake." Though his words pain me, I cannot ask any more of him. Not yet. I have not yet earned the right.

I follow him and Mariette inside and I help him lay her down on the bed. Her eyes flutter closed once more and though her face is still pale form the previous blood loss, her breathing is steady.

"She will be safe, Roselle. I promise you." Lorcan watches me as I look up from my inspection of my distant niece.

"She has to be, Lorcan." The words are wrenched from deep within me.

He pulls me away from the bed and over to the window, and I relish his touch. "I will send word to my contact and after Mariette has had a few more hours to recover, I shall get her safely on her way back to England."

I stare up at him. "You are very magnanimous," I say, hardly even daring to believe that he would do this for me, but perhaps it isn't for me, after all. Perhaps, he merely seeks to do what is just. As he once did for Coralie. That, I concede, is a far superior reason.

He looks as though he wishes to take me in his arms, or perhaps I wistfully imagine it, but instead he slowly releases my hand. "Lock the door after me," he says. "I will not be gone long. But admit no one. *No one*, Roselle."

After a moment, I nod. I wonder if Ines will seek me out, but I will do as Lorcan bids. I owe him this much. "I promise," I tell him, and he dips his head in a swift brush of his lips across my brow. So swift I think I imagined it.

I blink and he is already at the door. "Lock it after me," he repeats and leaves me in the chamber. Alone, with the only family I have left.

I lock the door, then move one of the chairs to the bedside, intent on a silent vigil of Mariette. I commit every one of her features to memory, as I once did with Nisette. Tears push from my eyes and I leave them to cascade down my cheeks. All sacrifices must come with a price. This pain shall be mine.

Mariette is so like me, I wonder if it would have caused Nisette pain to look upon her countenance. Would she have perhaps seen a ghost from her past, in the face of her progeny? Perhaps it is some mercy, my sister passed on before ever meeting Mariette, but that notion does not provide me with relief. *I* should never have met her either.

I am sobbing openly now, head bowed. A small hand alights on my arm, startling me.

"Do not cry, my lady." Mariette is sitting up in the bed; blue-green eyes kind. But it should be I who comforts her.

I dash away the tears. "I am well, Mariette, please do not worry yourself. How do you feel?"

She frowns in thought, one hand reaching up to her neck. Apprehensively, I track the movement with my gaze, but after a moment her expression clears. "How strange, I thought I recalled a pain in my neck, but it seems to have gone now. I just feel a trifle weary. Shall we be home soon? I declare, I could sleep for a week—but there is much to plan. I am to be married in a few weeks." She looks around the room in interest.

I force a smile, and a nod. "Yes, soon. I promise."

She leans back against the cushions. "That is good." She appears troubled for a moment. "I am longing to see Daniel." She plucks at the bedclothes in an anxious gesture.

"And I am certain he shall be most eager to be reunited with you," I tell her and when a beautiful smile graces her face, I am pleased she has obviously found a love match. Though, how we are to account for her absence, I have no notion. I hope Lorcan will have thought of that.

"I hope so, I do miss him," she says sleepily, before her eyes flutter closed once more.

Guilt and trepidation force me to stand and pace. Poor, sweet, Mariette. *Please*, I pray—to what deity, I know not—*please, ensure her safe return to those who love her*.

To distract myself, I walk over to the wardrobe and pull it open. I am surprised to find it full of gowns. Most are in the dark colours favoured by the court. I note one or two in my preferred purple, and black. For me, I am still in a kind of mourning, and will be wearing those colours over the midnight-blue and wine-red. I carry on my inspection and find a few gowns in paler hues, and I am immediately transported back to my debutante days.

Nisette's girlish giggles fill my mind and I see us poring over bolts of shimmering pink, white, and muted gold fabrics, choosing just the right one for the

Lamont Ball; the ball I first encountered Lorcan. If I concentrate really hard, I can almost feel the touch of the soft silks and organza. Oh, what a cruel mistress remembrance is; I alternately cherish, and abhor it.

I close the doors of the wardrobe, effectively cutting off the memory too. No good will come of wandering down the avenues of my mind. First, I must focus on getting Mariette to safety, only then can I concentrate on what has become my secondary goal, revenge.

I resume my seat, and wait patiently for Lorcan to return. Being patient is something I have become very adept at. I still everything within me, closing my eyes for a brief moment, yet keeping alert to the sounds of his returning knock.

I do not know how long it takes, but I am immediately out of my chair when it does come, accompanied by his soft, "Roselle, it is I."

I admit him, and he slides in like a dark shadow, and hastens to lock the door behind him. His face is grim.

"Were you unsuccessful?" I ask, my stillness evaporating.

He scrubs a hand over his face. "No, no… do not worry. I just ran into a few old friends and remembered why I loathe this existence so."

The way he says *friends*, makes me believe they are anything but.

We move away from the closed door.

"We must brave the dawn. My contact can get Mariette on the late morning ship but she must be in a carriage within the hour."

I nod. I will brave anything to ensure her safety. "How will we explain where she has been?"

"That is all in hand, but come. Don your heaviest cloak, we must make haste."

I have no luggage with me, so I re-fasten the cloak I arrived in and join Lorcan as he hefts Mariette into his arms.

I open the door and peer out into the corridor. This close to dawn, it appears empty, most seemingly settled in their rooms.

"Turn left; there is a servants' staircase," Lorcan directs me quietly, and I move down the long carpeted hallway, Lorcan carrying Mariette close behind.

"The doorway in front of you," he whispers and I pull it open.

A figure looms in the shadows and I let out a muffled screech as my hands clamp over my mouth to silence myself.

It is too late, we have been discovered.

Chapter FIFTEEN

My fear does not lessen, even when the figure reveals itself to be the ethereal-looking woman who had stood beside Duc LaCroix when we arrived—Katerin, I recall Elize calling her.

"Do not be afraid," she says in a soft, French accent. "I have been sent to assist you."

I exchange a look with Lorcan, who appears as surprised as I feel.

Katerin makes an exasperated noise, her eyes dancing with amusement. "Anaïs said to tell you '*liberté*'."

Lorcan's face clears. "All is well, Rose. We can trust her."

"Madame Roselle, I am Katerin," she says as I turn to her with a relieved expression.

"Hello, Katerin, I am pleased to make your acquaintance," I say, and she smiles at me.

"*Oui*, let us make haste." She turns on her heel, her bronze gown beneath her dark-brown cloak brushing on the steps in a whisper as we descend the staircase. She leads us out into a corridor and along it to a kitchen full of bustling compelled servants, who pay us no attention.

We carry on through them and out of a door leading into a kitchen garden. Through this and beneath the pale-navy sky, we make our way over to a gate, which Katerin unlocks with a key taken from the pocket of her cloak.

"Come," Katerin says, and leads us along the alleyway behind the chateau and onto a quiet street. The gentle whinny of horses reach my ears and I see a black carriage stands at the end of the street, with a few figures waiting next to it.

The smaller one detaches itself and steps forward into a patch of moonlight. I take in her face as she lowers her hood, and, with a start, I see she is an older version of the lovely Katerin.

"Mistress Anaïs," Lorcan says in a respectful tone.

"My lord, and who is this beauty?" Anaïs looks at me with curious amber eyes.

"My wife, Lady Roselle," Lorcan replies, "and this is Mariette, for whom we seek safe passage."

"Hello," I say.

"Lady Roselle," Anaïs says and dips a curtsy, perhaps noticing my thoughtful expression, she adds,

"And you have met my daughter, Katerin."

"Of course, forgive me, Mademoiselle Katerin, I should have noted the likeness at once," Lorcan says. "Anaïs had no children when last we met."

Katerin's eyes once again dance with amusement. "Fear sometimes clouds even the most perceptive eyes," she says lightly.

Lorcan gives a smile at that while Anaïs gestures to the carriage. "Time changes many things, my lord. Come, let us not linger. As you court-members say, dawn approaches. Let me introduce you to my son, Maxim."

We follow her over to the carriage and the gentleman with cognac-coloured hair pulls open the carriage door, and Lorcan settles Mariette inside on the plush seats.

Anaïs looks to me now. "Maxim has business in London. He shall escort Mariette and see her safely returned to the heart of her family."

My eyes flick to the gentleman, as handsome as his sister is lovely. He regards me steadily back with his amber-coloured eyes. I cannot help show some trepidation. I do not know this man. How can I trust Mariette's safety to a stranger?

Anaïs' hand settles on my arm. "Fear not, my lady. Maxim will protect her. He is one of the most powerful warlocks in our coven."

"Coven?" I ask in surprise. "Then you are not…" I trail off, unknowing how to refer to what Lorcan and I are. What I call us in our head will not be deemed as respectful.

Understanding flickers in Anaïs' gaze. Had she perhaps caught my disgust? "No, my dear, we are immortal, but not in the same way as yourselves."

I look to Lorcan, but his gaze his unreadable. I have moved in this darkened world for a century, yet I still do not truly know it.

"Then how is Katerin part of Duc LaCroix's court?" I suddenly do not know if we are putting our trust in those who would seek to betray us.

"I am an emissary to the duc. We work closely together to ensure the court and coven exist in harmony; no harm is to come to any in our coven, and we in turn assist with spells and special potions."

Dizziness swamps me, and a metallic tang cloys the back of my throat. *A special spell, tethering Lorcan and I for a century.* I press one hand to my brow.

"Are you well?" Anaïs asks gently.

"I—I…" I cannot speak, I cannot look at Lorcan.

"Maman, it shall be sunrise soon," Katerin's soft voice breaks through my stupor, and I try desperately to pull some semblance of myself back together.

"Say your goodbyes, Rose," Lorcan says gruffly.

I give a jerky nod, before climbing up into the carriage. I stroke one gentle hand over Mariette's hair as she slumbers. "Be safe, my dear niece. Live your life fully and boldly," I tell her, a sob catching in my throat. I turn away and step out. Maxim assists me down. "Please, look after her," I implore him.

"I vow it," he responds, and I believe him. It is if his words are some kind of spell themselves.

"You need not worry yourself, my lady. Maxim will weave a protection spell, and into it will be the truth that she has spent time in Paris with family" — Anaïs smiles at me — "to buy things for her trousseau. Anyone she comes in contact with will believe it, and the story will spread and become fact. Her reputation and her life will be safe."

"How can we ever repay you?" I ask, moved beyond belief at the length the coven will go to ensure the safety of one unknown girl.

Anaïs ponders me, amber eyes gleaming deep. "Maybe our wants shall converge. There is a reason the mutual truce was put in place. One of ours was attacked and changed, and now lives as you do, though she does not want that life. Perhaps, if you can find a way to help her, our debt shall be repaid. But even if you cannot help, we shall still protect your Mariette. We need more light in this world."

"I will do all I can," I vow myself, and feel the weight of the words. Though they have no actual or true magic behind them, they have a kind of magic all of their own; the magic of sincerity.

"I believe you," Anaïs says, then turns to Lorcan. "Might I have a word?" Lorcan nods and they turn to one side.

With a respectful nod to Katerin who goes forward to speak with her brother, I wander over to an alcove and ponder Anaïs' words, questioning who else it is that I need to help. *Maybe our wants shall converge.* With a shiver, I wonder if the other woman can see into my mind, to the hard pit inside me named Revenge.

I add another layer over the pitted stone and my thoughts turn to Mariette. I had secured a century for Nisette, how long would Mariette's protection last?

"My dear, something troubles you." Anaïs has silently joined me. Taking my hand, she leads me into a covered archway. "Mariette is out of danger. She has safe passage home, and protection. She shall remember none of this nightmare."

"But for how long?" I nibble my lip, my eyes trailing over to the carriage as if I can see inside to where Mariette is concealed; slumber shielding her. I thought I had secured enough protection for Nisette, but the sands of time ran out, and with it, her line's defences.

Anaïs smiles as I look back at her; a touch of arrogance colours it. "I am far more powerful than I seem, my lady, as too is Maxim. Mariette and all who follow after her will be hidden from those who seek to hunt them, and hurt them. And hunt them they would, because she is of a pure soul line, the same as you."

I blink at her. "You are mistaken, Mistress Anaïs, there is only darkness within me. I battle it every single moment," the last comes out as a tortured whisper.

She once again takes my hand, looking deep into my eyes; amber to green. "No. You are mistaken. That is why purer souls have it so much harder... because they must *battle* harder. The darkness is drawn to their light... it craves it... seeks it... yearns to devour it. That is why pure souls suffer, because they live that battle every single day. A battle not fought with sword and shield, but with light, love, and kindness." I feel her words deep within me, almost painfully. "For their souls are the sweetest prize, and so they are the ones most sought after. Dark souls are easy prey, but taste bitter on the tongue. An empty, hollow succour that does not sustain... imagine how long one night creature could feed off a bright shining soul, my lady. *Imagine*."

I do not want to imagine such horror, but still,

what she speaks I comprehend acutely. Why corrupt the already corrupted? The yield from those filled with light would be a far appetising win. Nausea roils through me.

"That is why they sought you. That is why you cannot let them have what is left of your light. Be the candle in the darkness, Lady Roselle. You alone may hold the balance in your hands. *Your* light could be the one that tips the balance. Far more is at stake than you could even possibly fathom. Do not give up." Anaïs squeezes my hands. "Do not *ever* give up."

I feel emotionally wrecked. I have always believed I am nothing but a vessel for shadows and death, but could the coven leader be correct; is that why I continue to fight? Does the light still glimmer inside me?

All I can do is hope what she speaks is truth, and find a way to keep fighting. There must be a way to free Lorcan and I from this, and the other unfortunate Anaïs spoke of.

"I won't give up, Mistress," I say and she nods at me, satisfied.

"You are strong, my lady. Have faith that you will find a way and once you discover it, use your light to illuminate the path."

"Thank you… sincerely, for all you have done for my family." I lean in and hug her, and she hugs me back.

"I have faith that you will free far more than yourself and your husband," she says enigmatically, before she smiles at me and glides back over to the carriage to speak to Maxim. They briefly converse before he slides into the carriage and the coachman urges the horses on, headed for the faraway port.

I silently say my final goodbyes, knowing I will never see Mariette again, but truly that is as it ought. The dead and the living should never encounter each other on the same plane. I am witness to the catastrophic aftermath.

I thoughtfully watch Anaïs and Katerin leave—blending seamlessly into the shadows—my mind a riot of questions and possibilities.

"Are you well?" Lorcan is by my side, and looking down at me.

I smile softly. "I cannot explain it but I feel hope for the first time in an extremely long time."

Lorcan's eyes kindle. "You do?"

My eyes meet his. "Yes. Mayhap it has to do with seeing Mariette safely off, but what if this is just the catalyst to more things changing? I feel as though we are winning somehow."

"Winning? What?"

The battle for our souls, I want to say, but would

he think me nonsensical? I dip my head, suddenly bashful. "Oh, pay me no mind. I am in a peculiar mood today."

"I like this side of you, Roselle. It is reminiscent of when we first met, when you were vibrant with hopes and dreams for your future. A future I longed to be a part of."

Lorcan's words has my new fledgling hope faltering.

"Oh, Lorcan. I so wished that for us. How cruel fate was; teasing us with what could never have been."

"No, do not speak like that, Rose, there is still a chance, and back then we would have had a chance too. I was trying to find a way to free myself so I could be with you."

"But fate intervened and stole that chance," I murmur, eyes staring off into the distance.

Lorcan takes my upper arms, forcing me to look at him. "This time, we shall steal it back, my love."

My hope returns in a rush at his words. He still wishes to try. "Yes, my love," I say. "Yes."

His eyes enflame with blue heat and then he is taking my lips with his, and in a darkened alcove on a Parisian street, I re-find my fight. Lorcan is the blacksmith, smiting tiny weapons upon my lips, weapons of strength, purpose, and hope. I feel them sink into my skin, fortifying my armour.

We have more allies than I thought on our side. Mayhap we can indeed steal back that chance. If there is even the merest possibility, then we must at least try.

Lorcan makes a noise deep in his throat, and deepens the kiss, before he breaks it off suddenly. "Let us return to the chateau before we are missed and hunted down, my love, Katerin has gone on ahead to ensure us safe admittance. We must rest in preparation for the Midnight Picnic tonight... and then we shall continue this." His smile is all promise.

I smile up at him. With my husband by my side, I can participate in anything requested of me.

"Yes," I say. "Let us not tarry. Dawn approaches." I do not even need to glance up at the lilac sky to know. I feel it dancing beneath my skin, little pinpricks of warning.

Lorcan nods, adjusting my hood, before tucking me close beside him and leading me back to the chateau; just two shades keeping to the shadows.

Mariette is safe.

Happiness swells inside me. Now the next stage of my plan can begin, but now it is *our* plan. Hope, shining, hope, follows me in through the kitchen door just as the first deadly daggers of dawn slice the garden behind us.

This time I shall not cower from the light, but embrace it. The tiny flicker of light inside of me is the only weapon I have against the darkness.

As Lorcan takes my hand and leads me back up the servants' staircase, his smile is bright too.

And, that, I shall embrace also.

It shines for me.

And I? I blaze for him.

Chapter Sixteen

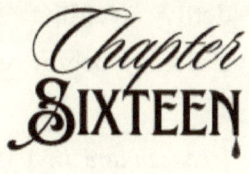

"Stay close beside me and all shall be well, my love," Lorcan whispers to me, and I nod, my eyes wide on the sights around me.

Katerin, Ines, and Valdis had worked together and wove spells to create a bountiful-yet-frozen garden. Purple-black roses with thick pungent scents line the walkway through a courtyard and out beyond into the vast garden, bleeding into blood-red flowers. They blanket the grass, bespelled to stay blooming and fragrant for the duration of the days' long revelry.

The Midnight Picnic is the first official event, followed by parties and ending with the centennial ball in two nights.

I can scarcely believe we are on the cusp of not just a new year, but a new century. How magical would it be to start it anew and erase the last century? But that is not to be—what a fanciful notion.

Raucous laughter greets my ears, and Lorcan turns me away from a candlelit gazebo, aiming for a rose-covered bower, deftly avoiding the other court members who have already begun celebrating in their own sordid way.

I can do this. I can endure it, I think and look to Lorcan as he settles me on the bench beneath the bower. He stands sentry beside me, as though warning all others away. He stiffens.

"It is all right," I say as I recognise Ines walking over to us; her long deep-blue dress dragging over the flowers, lifting their scents into the air. "It is only my friend, Ines." As I stare at her, a thought strikes me. Was Ines from Anaïs' coven?

"My lord, my lady." She gives a delicate curtsy. Over her shoulder, I notice Katerin gliding across the grass, but I am not the only one who watches her; Adair's gaze is hungry as he stands beside Duke Lamont and Duc LaCroix with Draven the other side and observes her approach. Katerin joins them and I refocus on Ines as Lorcan speaks to her.

"Hello again, Ines. I never thanked you for your assistance on the ship. I was not myself."

She dips her head. "I am happy to be of assistance to you both," she says. She leans closer. "And I understand you were successful in getting her safely away."

Here is my segue. "We were... your coven was

most helpful," I say, going with instinct.

Her eyes widen imperceptibly, then she nods. "Unfortunately, I am no longer a part of the coven."

I sit back in surprise. Surely, Anaïs would not cast Ines out?

"I left by choice," Ines explains. "In the beginning I thought I might be a danger to my brothers and sisters. I asked Duc LaCroix for sanctuary, and he granted it... until I was sent to England to assist Valdis." She flicks a look at a still Lorcan, then back to me, her gaze apologetic.

"But was it not Duc LaCroix's court that changed you?" My curiosity at her story helps me overcome the flinch at the mention of the reason she was sent to England. Ines' expression changes in an instant, and I regret my thoughtless question. "Ines, I am sorry—" I begin, but she rallies and spares me a smile.

"It is all right, Roselle. We all three share a common sire, I am afraid."

Unconsciously, my gaze wanders over to that of Duke Lamont, who tosses back the contents of the goblet he holds, then imperiously waves one of the compelled servants over to re-fill it. My flinch is more of a shudder this time.

"My father?" Lorcan says, distaste evident in his tone.

Ines nods. "Yes, he visited Paris and demanded an audience with Anaïs' coven. No pact had been brokered then. When she would not agree to his demands, he sought punishment. Unfortunately, it was I who was the first member of her coven found. He left me broken and almost drained on her doorstep, but had fed me some of his blood; I can only imagine he hoped my turning would wreak death upon them all."

"No," I gasp out, hand to my mouth.

"I was too late to be saved. I turned, and left my coven."

"So that is why you came up with the potion to stave off the thirst, and the one to help regenerate mortal blood for those inflicted?"

Her lips twist uncomfortably. "Yes, but unfortunately word of my prowess reached my sire; not *what* I was working on, but just my skill, perhaps enhanced because of my new status. He convinced Duc LaCroix to allow him to take me back to England with him. They had an argument over it, until Duke Lamont reminded him that as my sire he ultimately had the power to take me without Duc LaCroix's blessing."

"They had a dispute, did they?" Lorcan says musingly, his gaze thoughtful as he watches his father and the duc.

"Indeed. From what I gather, the pact with Anaïs

and Duc LaCroix happened soon after."

"That is very interesting," Lorcan says.

"I am sorry that happened to you, Ines," I say, standing and taking one of her slender hands in my own. "If I could but help you, then I shall endeavour to find a way." Knowing it truly was Ines that Anaïs had referred to, solidified my intent. I must find a way to help her.

I look up to find Duke Lamont staring straight at us. His gaze pierces right into the very core of me, before he raises his goblet in a mocking toast and drinks it all down.

"I should go, we do not want him to grow suspicious," Ines says, "but know that you have more allies than you might think within this court." She drops another curtsy to us both, then melts away, seemingly blending into the foliage.

I turn to Lorcan, intent on discussing this revealing information, feeling confident with our new-found closeness. Brokered by our shared success at spiriting Mariette safely away, and our subsequent heartfelt declarations, the feeling that we are winning somehow returns with a passion.

But, in an instant, the feeling disappears at the expression on his face. I falter backwards to sit heavily on the bench.

All the light in his smile—the one he had turned my way when we arrived back at the chateau—is gone. Instead to be replaced by a cold, haughty look as he turns to look down at me.

"Your companion has arrived," he tells me in a voice that could have been pulled from the depths of hades itself.

I try to stand, I do, but my legs will not support me. *No*. I feel it all slipping away, everything we have worked so hard to achieve today is gone. Gone because of the arrival of the one who betrayed me. Who Lorcan believes I *chose* to spend my own confinement with. I can only imagine what the duke told him, and I still have yet to explain my side. But now, I fear, he will not hear it.

I turn hurt eyes upon Lorcan. "He is dead to me," I utter, and the irony is not lost on me, but still I somehow manage to stand and, gathering the skirts of my deep purple gown, I hurry away from him. Away from his accusing gaze.

I do not look in the duke's party's direction, though I feel the heavy weight of a new observation upon me. One I recognise. I should; I felt it for one hundred years.

Inside the chateau, I find a secluded spot on a tufted seat set before a shadowy alcove. A window opposite allows in a modicum of moonlight, and I take comfort from its silvery light. I will not cry. Not this time.

Oh, what a cruel conductor Yves Lamont is. Making me choose between my new husband and my sister, enforcing a century's long confinement with my betrayer, whispering noxious hints about my conduct into Lorcan's ears, and now, just as we are seemingly growing closer again, he waves his baton and Lirrel enters, right on cue.

"Roselle?"

I close my eyes at Lorcan's voice. Of course he found me. He will always find me.

"I am here, Lorcan," I say, though I know he can scent me.

He moves closer and leans against the wall of the alcove.

"Do you remember that night we first met, Rose? Do you?"

"Of course I do, Lorcan. How could I ever forget." My voice is near to breaking as I recall that first meeting.

Lorcan's face is in half-shadow, but I can feel the tension radiating off him.

"And do you remember me warning you away from the gardens?"

I bite my lip, recalling the whimpering, mewling sounds. I nod, suddenly unable to speak. He moves from the shadows and prowls closer.

"*If* you had ventured within, you would have seen Lirrel's true character then; the depth of his depravity. He, alone, was responsible for far more debutantes' innocent blood being supped than any other, even my father."

Bile burns my throat. "But… but I had just danced with him moments before I decided to venture outside." I cannot think clearly.

I stood so close to a thirsting monster long before I ever knew him for what he was—a monster with an angelic friend's face—and actually enjoyed his company. Long before he was my century-long companion, he was put forward by my father as a prospective *suitor*. Not that I saw him in that way. But I thought, perhaps, Nisette, would consider Lirrel. The horror intensifies at that forgotten fact resurfacing.

Nisette, sweet Nisette, and Lirrel supping on her in the garden like countless others. Nausea burns through me at my imaginings. *Burns.*

I was nought but a plaything in his sick, twisted games. My family, casualties of his triumph. The thought is a bitter pill to swallow. But to know now that Lirrel had *always* been a beast, right from the very beginning, is worse. He groomed me until I *trusted* him with all our lives. I *confided* in him about my love for Lorcan. He encouraged my confidences with a sympathetic ear.

Had he intended to turn me for himself? But when he discovered my love for Lorcan, did he see an opportunity to best Lorcan and put himself in the duke's good graces?

I fear it was both all along.

I stumble away from the seat over to the window. Away from Lorcan and the truth he speaks, my hand clutching at my throat. Does he know it causes me unbearable agony? Does he—in his jealousy—even care?

"Do you think I don't know *now* what he is, Lorcan? There is no need to warn me of his nature thus. Your warning comes one hundred years too late." I shake my head, trying to dislodge the tiny hammers of pain. How can he not know that I have vowed revenge upon my former friend? "You cannot think me so naïve as to believe him my friend. Was *ever* my true friend. You were *there* at Castle Lamont. There, when your father revealed all. You bore witness to my reaction."

"But before you knew the truth you still spent one *hundred* years with him, Roselle. You left Castle Lamont with him *willingly*. An intimate party of two. What else

189

am I to think?" Lorcan follows me, and I cannot tell if he is furious or heartbroken—perhaps, the two emotions are so closely intertwined that the difference is insignificant. Back and forth we go in this green-eyed dance. How can we move on? How can I make him see that all I thought of was him? Only him. I would have, without question, spent that century alone if I had known Lirrel bore the responsibility for our tragic situation.

But yet, I cannot blame Lorcan for his anger towards me. I feel its equivalent at myself. Perhaps it even surpasses it. "You are right, I deserve this and more. So much more." My voice cracks.

"Rose, I did not mean—" but we are interrupted as Adair appears before us.

"Your presence is requested by His Grace." He smiles coldly, and I know it isn't a mere request. Yves Lamont's requests are always a ducal summons in disguise. *Not now, please*. I cannot take any more assault on my emotional state.

Lorcan is immediately by my side and, despite the fraught tension between us, takes my arm solicitously. Though my feet are leaden, he escorts me back outside, Adair following.

"Ah, my children, there you are. You must welcome dear Lirrel properly. You, especially Roselle, are old friends, are you not?" Oh, how I despise the duke in this very moment, from the depths of his amused smirk, to the blackened maw of his empty soul.

The duke claps a hand to Lirrel's shoulder, who has the audacity to look into my eyes as if he knows not that all I wish is to claw his out. He appears as I remember, but with a hardened, polished edge, like black obsidian.

Lorcan's arm tenses where mine is looped through his, and I must do all I can not to react.

"Of—of course. Good evening, Lirrel," I say, my voice hollow. Lirrel smirks in response. All trace of the cowardly, cowering version I saw in Castle Lamont's ballroom erased.

"Tsk, tsk, where is my effervescent daughter-in-law? Come now, Lirrel tells me you are light of foot. Valentin and I must see you both dance together." The duke looks from me to Lirrel, the smirk on his face widening.

Duc LaCroix watches me intently. I cannot make a misstep in his court, and to snub the duke's request in front of Valentin LaCroix... well, punishment would be swift. Of course, I have no choice.

When have I ever had a true choice in any of this?

Chapter
SEVENTEEN

Resigned to my fate, I go to remove my arm from Lorcan's, but he holds it tighter against his side. The duke laughs, but it is bloated with warning. "Come now, Lorcan. Did I not always tell you to *share*? She will be in your sight."

Lorcan and his father stare at one another for one long, red-rimmed moment, before Lorcan breaks the gaze and releases me, bowing over my hand. He does not meet my eyes, and oh, how I wish he would. I need to convey to him, that I only wish to dance in *his* embrace forever more.

But he releases me and strides to his father's side, and Lirrel stands before me. He takes my hand in his own long slender-fingered one as the first ethereal strains of a haunting tune begins playing from the gazebo. I falter at the once-familiar tune, and Lirrel's smile turns sharp as I stare up at him in mute fury. He leads me over to the outside dance floor set upon mosaic stone slabs and takes me in hold, spinning me out into the dancing throng in a dizzying whirl. He is enjoying every macabre moment.

"*Do not speak to me*," I tell him through frozen lips, turning my face away from the two dukes and the watchful gaze of my husband as we pass them. I cannot bear to witness Lorcan's reaction. That is, if he even watches us at all. At that thought, I cannot help but seek him out on the flower-strewn edge of the dancefloor, and my lips part as I take in his livid, yet almost mask-like, face.

Lirrel takes the opportunity to lean in, his lips close to my neck and murmur, "Oh, but this is so much fun, my lady. I simply must claim your attention, and how else but recollections of the past. Our past."

I jerk my head backwards, uncaring if the duke sees me. "How dare you," I hiss. "There is no '*our*' anything. It was all an illusion, of your making."

"One hundred years we shared, see how it pains your husband to know that he only had mere days with you." He whirls me around, directly placing us in Lorcan's eyeline.

My eyes skitter over his face, the horror and terror warring within me at Lirrel's statement. Lorcan appears hewn from granite, and I yearn to go to him before any more damage can be wrought, but Lirrel grasps me almost painfully by the waist. We continue on, my footsteps wanting to drag. That is when I see it. The monster Lirrel truly is. The one that lurked in the hedge maze that night over a hundred years ago. The monster that waited for me, if I had been folly enough to sate my curiosity, as he sated his thirst.

Almost impassively now, I fulfil my role, and dance; light of foot, and grace and beauty imbued. Not a willing participant, but willing to do whatever it takes to get through this charade and be back at my husband's side.

The music thankfully ends and the duke looks delighted as Lirrel bows over my hand. "I do hope we shall find the time to properly reconcile, my lady." His tone is mocking, his eyes leaping with mirth.

Oh, how I was indeed deceived. *This* is the true Lirrel. I never knew him at all.

I count the steps until we reach Lorcan's side and I immediately press myself up against his side, seeking comfort from him, but stone-like, he doesn't even acknowledge me.

"*Charmante*, Roselle," Valentin says, and I meet his eyes. I almost startle when I see a genuine kindness in his ancient gaze.

I curtsy. "*Merci*," I murmur and he smiles. One without fangs.

"Indeed, dear, daughter-in-law. Simply charming. I

am so gladdened to see two old friends reunited in such a pleasing way." Yves leans in towards me, and I force myself to hold still and not flinch away. *Do not show fear. Do not show weakness.*

"*Oui*, now Lirrel, you must allow me to introduce you to Katerin. She is my most trusted guard and emissary. Accompany us, Yves." Valentin nods at Lorcan and I, and draws both the duke and Lirrel away, with Lirrel tossing us a mocking look over his shoulder. Adair and Draven trail after them towards where Katerin now converses with Valdis.

"I am going to kill him. And I shall enjoy doing it." Lorcan's voice is full of a dark promise and startles me in to looking up at him.

"Lorcan, I—"

"Let us be gone from this cursed place," Lorcan interrupts me, and suddenly he is pulling me by the hand, weaving us around dancing couples and pleasure-seeking clusters.

He doesn't stop propelling us on until we are ensconced inside his bedchamber with the door locked behind us. Only then does he let go of my hand, but simply to stalk away and stare mutely out of the tall windows, framed by billowing gossamer drapes.

"Lorcan, please, talk to me." I settle a dainty hand on his shoulder, and feel hope when he does not flinch away from me.

"I have no care to talk," he growls, and I slowly remove my hand, intent on removing myself from his chamber also, but before I have even taken a step away he has whirled around and captured me in his firm embrace. "But I do want this…" He lowers his face into my neck, and desire shoots through me in one bright shining spear.

Yes.

His fangs graze my skin, each touch an electric jolt of sensation, and my own lengthen in response. Pain, exquisite pain, accompanies the transformation.

"Do you want me, Roselle? Do you want this as much as I?" Lorcan rasps against my neck, and I moan.

"You know I do, Lorcan, you know I could never resist you… even from the very first."

"Then say it."

"*I want you*, Lorcan." The words are barely from my lips before he lifts me and carries me over to his bed, laying me down as if I were an offering. And I am. I offer myself up to my husband, and he in turn will worship at my alter. Down on his knees, he pushes up the skirts of my gown, the sound a seductive whisper in the darkness, the only noise that fills the room.

His hands hesitate at the apex to my thighs, and I thrust my hands into his hair, forcing him to look at me.

His eyes are hooded, but I see what I want to see… he feels as I do. This tumult inside us can only be sated in this way. Words are cast aside in favour of actions, and in this very moment I have no care for them either.

My eyes do the talking… *come to me…*

His own eyes flare and he lowers himself to me, and moments later we are one, riding the wave of the turbulence we have wrought. But it is one I welcome, because finally I am *feeling.* If we could but stay like this for eternity. I could endure an existence such as this. It would be all I need to endure. Rapture, sweet rapture, in a world of chaos.

I feel myself coming undone, and I capture Lorcan's gaze once again, needing the connection to be complete… as I am replete.

I fracture; ripple after ripple spans the length and breadth of my body as Lorcan moves above me, uttering my name like a prayer. But it is I who should revere him. He has given me this. A gift far beyond my deserving.

He shudders once, twice, then his mouth captures mine in one long searing kiss. I cling to him. To the knowledge that whatever else happens, we shall always have this. A frozen glass bubble in time where we can always find our own sanctuary within one another's embrace.

He draws his mouth away to trail hot kisses down the column of my neck, and I arch beneath him. Despite my completion, it is suddenly not enough. I want to bind myself to him, body, and whatever is left of my soul, so that we are never separated again.

"Lorcan—"

"Hush, my love." He runs one large hand down my face, closing my eyes. "Try to rest." He tucks me into his arms, his chin resting on the top of my head, and though dawn is still some hours away, I find myself drifting away to the dark dwelling where nightmares take the place of dreams. But this time I am not alone.

I face them, isolated no longer...

..."Dance with me," Lirrel holds out one slender-fingered hand, a boyish smile on his frozen-in-time face.

I cannot help but smile back. "You are in a merry mood," I observe, and I too feel something akin to contentedness for the first time in a long time.

After many long years, we have found our rhythm; resting by day, and indulging in a semblance of society life at night, although our party of two should make for a monotony. But I enjoy the protection of the routine. The replaying of the same day over and over serves to help me forget what I have done. Instead I can pretend, that everything is as it ought and Lirrel is a friend, whose role is to be my platonic companion, as I am his.

"Very well," I say, and I note the surprise in his eyes.

"You honour me, my lady," he says as I stand and accept his hand.

He swallows as he takes me in hold. He nods to the hazy-eyed footman, who sits and begins tinkling out a tune on the pianoforte. He whirls me around and the ballroom spins around me in a flash of muted colours. A laugh bursts from me, surprising both Lirrel and myself.

"It makes me gladdened to see your beautiful face alight with such joy," he tells me huskily and captures my gaze.

Something shifts inside me, a candle snuffing out, as his words seep in. I falter, my steps mismatching his, and we stop. I pull away. This is not right.

"Thank you for the dance," I tell him in a dull voice, turning away.

"My lady!" he calls after me as I hurry from the room, the sound of the footman still playing the jaunty tune ghosting my retreat.

A hand clamps on my shoulder as Lirrel catches up to me and turns me to face him, his eyes—now with a reddened halo—searching mine.

I fight against the hold. Suddenly unable to bear being touched. Touch evokes feeling and I deserve neither touch nor feeling.

"No," I moan, but the grip intensifies...

..."Roselle, hush, I am here... I am here."

I awake and find the hand gripping me is not one I should flinch from, but one I long for.

"Lorcan?" I ask, hardly daring to believe he is still there, that he has not deserted me while I slept.

"Who else?" he utters, and I instinctively shy back. He makes a frustrated noise. "I am sorry, that was ungentlemanly."

"There is only you. There has only ever been you. And if I lived without you for a millennia more there would only *ever* be you," I state huskily, and his eyes widen, before they shutter.

He does not believe me, and yet I cannot blame him. I am no more judge than he is my executioner. But I am determined to earn his trust, his love, and all that goes with it. I begin now. I settle one hand against his cheek, and pour as much love into my gaze as I can evoke.

I lean up and press my lips to his. They remain immobile beneath mine for a moment more before they soften and we create our own version of heat. How paradoxical that two ice-cold bodies with frozen hearts can burn together with such intensity.

"You shall be my undoing," Lorcan murmurs against my lips. "You compelled me from that very first moment... Rose, my sweet dark Rose."

But it is I who is undone. I unravel in his arms, as though I am made from nothing but spun thread. Remnants of the fabric of my old life comes apart as my heart bursts open. For him. Only for him.

He knits me back together, stitch by tiny stitch, until I cover him. My love covers us both. I just hope it will be enough for now, until he rediscovers his own.

He pulls back. "I have been summoned," he says, and I blink up at him.

"How?" I say, but the heavy knock at the door drowns out my words.

A wry smile twists at Lorcan's lips. Of course, where I hide away from my preternatural 'gifts', Lorcan has had centuries to hone his own.

I sit up against the plush cushions. After a sudden promise-filled kiss, Lorcan moves away from me and straightens his trousers and shirt before donning his long boots.

"Stay," he says, "rest as long as you need."

A tentative smile frames my lips. "Thank you," I murmur.

He opens the door and is gone before I even blink.

Every muscle in my body feels loose and boneless and I think that even if I wanted to, I would not be able to move. So I do not. Instead, I slide down until I am nestled in the tangled silken covers and surrounded by Lorcan's intoxicating scent. I smooth one cheek against the material, like a feline leaving its fragrance. Perhaps when Lorcan returns, he will smell me here, and take comfort.

Although I fear what other nightmarish memories may surface in my sleep, I do not hesitate in closing my eyes once again. Lorcan wants me here, so I shall stay and indulge in rest while I can.

For I still have plans of my own. Revenge awaits. Thank darkness, there is no deadline, only perhaps one of my own making.

With that thought in mind, a smile curves my lips as I hope to succumb once more to the velvety abyss of slumber.

Chapter
EIGHTEEN

Slumber is, as I feared, elusive—it is still night after all—and I cannot rest. Despite knowing Lorcan wished me to stay in his bed, I decide to wander the chateau. This close to dawn, I will be safe from the attentions of others, and the servants pay me no mind. I move ghostlike through the halls until something compels me to push open the door to the covered stone walkway outside. Perhaps the hint of frost scenting the air reminds me of home. Of the moments where I would pay my respects and honour my parents and Nisette.

I lean against the stone wall, my gaze heavy on the courtyard visible through the arched openings. Twinned with the scent of frost evoking memories, I have always felt a kinship to this particular phase of time. The fragmented last moments of night, where the veil of noctem splinters away from the seeking fingers of Brigid. Fancifully, I imagine the goddess of the dawn, wielding her light like spears, striking at the darkness and driving it back for another day. If only I could stave back my own darkness thus.

The lavender light bathes the grey bricks in a soothing velvet pearlescent sheen, tempting me to step out into the courtyard. I yearn to run my hands over the stonework to see if it feels as I imagine it. But I make no move. To step out and linger now would be folly, even I, in my melancholy state, know this.

A whisper of movement beside me has me straightening in surprise. Elize stands beside me, her eyes distracted. But it is not her features which give me pause, it is her appearance; I have never seen her look less than perfectly put together and coiffured. Now, she wears a filmy nightgown of dusky grey lace, a silken robe draping at her shoulders, displaying creamy flesh, and a slender column of neck. Her hair is abundantly loose, in long roping coils, and floats around her shoulder to her waist in a heavy dark-brown swathe.

She turns and blinks her ice-blue eyes at me. She raises one hand and, instinctively, I flinch back, thinking she means to lash out, but she merely leans in and cups my face in a surprisingly motherly gesture.

"Dear, sweet, innocent Rose. You do all for love, but love… it is not worth it. Not in the end, and perhaps never in the beginning too." Her voice is dull, yet I can hear every ounce of pain vibrating through it.

Though I have no affection for the woman who has

taken great delight in tormenting me over the years, and stole Mariette away from her beautiful life to thrust her into a living nightmare, pity still somehow nudges me.

"Elize, let me escort you back to your chamber. You appear unwell." I take the hand, pressed against my cheek, in mine, but she removes it from my grip easily.

"Always trying to help those in pain, Roselle." Her smile is sad, a faded echo of her usual calculating sharp version. Lines bracket her mouth, as if the smile were an afterthought to the words. "I think I shall just stay here a moment longer. Dawn approaches. It has been such an age since I have witnessed its beauty."

Her words unsettle me, despite the innocuity of them. "Elize please." I go to take her hand once more, but she glides away from me and steps out into the courtyard, and now I know why I am unsettled. Her intent is clear. "Return to the walkway, Elize," I urge her.

She stands in the centre of the three curved stone benches, and throws me a solemn look over her shoulder, before tilting her face upwards, arms rising as if praising the coming sunlight. Sunlight which is now painting the gables surrounding the courtyard in pale copper.

If I am quick, I can reach her.

I take one step out, but I am pulled roughly back. "*No.*" The word is uttered harshly and I turn to see the livid blue gaze of the duke. No sooner has he pulled me back into the safe shadowy confines of the covered walkway, than a scream erupts behind us.

I turn in time to see Elize flooded in a golden light. And though her mouth is open in a piercing scream, she does not look to be in pain; her face is aglow with a rhapsodic expression. It morphs and twists as tiny embers flicker beneath her skin. I realise what is truly happening; she is being incinerated from within.

I look at the duke, at his grim expression. "We must help her!" I scream, and he flicks me an impatient, yet curious, look.

"It is too late. There is no helping her now," he says, but I cannot believe that. Surely, even Elize does not deserve this excruciating end? Perhaps, he senses something in my gaze because he looks beyond me and thrusts me backwards. "Take her away," he says, and I am enveloped in the familiar scent of my husband.

"Come, Roselle," Lorcan says, and tries to draw me away, but a sudden roar from the other end of the walkway has me pushing out of his hold.

"*Elize!*"

Adair runs along the walkway; his face a picture of

206

agonising grief. With a strength that surpasses even that of the duke, he launches himself away from Yves' gripping hold and rushes, without hesitation, out into the courtyard, sunlight flickering over his hair.

He reaches Elize, just as she explodes into a pile of glittering ash. His arms grasp at nothing, his cries echoing around the courtyard, as the same embers ignite him from inside of his body.

Now, I see an emotion on the duke's face as his cheekbones hollow in on themselves as he shouts, "You fool!"

Adair merely hangs his smouldering head, before dropping to his knees. His lava-limned hands splay out over Elize's remains, and then it is all over. He has joined her, and a light breeze casts them away in a swirling fusion.

The duke spins away from the scene, and now I am truly afraid, as the emotion I saw previously displayed intensifies into a grotesque, red-eyed rage. He ploughs his fist through one of the columns and the whole walkway shudders around us.

"Take. Her. Away," he pants and Lorcan once again turns my face into his chest, but not before I have seen the over-long fangs, and the claw-like nails extruding from the duke's hand that he slowly un-fists.

Lorcan wastes no time in blurring us away from

the horrific death arena.

I open my eyes and find we are in my chamber. "Oh, Lorcan," I manage before I am sobbing. How can I feel so much pain and sympathy for Elize and Adair; they have been nothing but cruel to me and so many others. Their machinations were cold and calculating, yet still, I cannot help myself.

"I am sorry, you should not have had to witness that," Lorcan murmurs against my hair as he holds me on his lap.

"But *why*? Why would she do that?" I ask, through my tears.

Lorcan pulls back and turns my face to his. "Because she believed she had lost Adair. That he no longer loved her." His tone is measured, but his eyes tell a different story. He understands Elize's perceived anguish. To my shame; he understands. But is wrong, so very wrong. Lorcan will never lose my affections. *Ever*.

"But he loved her, it was obvious to all, despite the fact that they were both free with their affections with others, they were a pair." I struggle to understand how Elize had come to such a conclusion, and to take such extreme measures because of it.

Lorcan inclines his head. "Most within the courts are fluid in their affections, it is true, and they both took advantage of that, but only ever with the other present. Never solitary with another. That was their unspoken rule, one that they both adhered to."

I flush at the insinuation, and my mind baffles at how such a feat could be achieved, and how two people who truly *loved* each other could even think about including another in such an intimate, love-affirming, sacred act. "But Adair did not... did he?" I thought back to the heated look exchanged between Katerin and Adair, and Elize's frozen expression, and how I believed there must have been history between the trio.

Lorcan strokes the hair back from my face, and shakes his head. "My father and I were walking the upper halls, when she passed us, mumbling incoherently. It was only after she blurred away that we came upon an anxious Adair, discovered she had found him with another, and comprehended the true state of her mind. We followed her scent, and my father reached you first, but by then it was too late. Something must have broken within her."

Yes. Her heart. Even one so cold and dead inside had a seed in her heart that could still break it seemed. And in this moment, I understand that immortality does not preclude love even for those who embrace the creature darkness creates. There must still be a sliver of light within them, for how else could they love otherwise?

"It was horrific. I tried to stop her. I did. I tried to stop her…" I break off, again crying. Crying for the mortal woman Elize once was, who had allowed love to change the very course of her life… and subsequently her death.

"Rose. Sweet, Rose," Lorcan peppers my forehead with kisses. "You cannot save everyone."

"What about us, Lorcan? Can we save us?" I search his face.

He stares silently back at me for one long moment, then, "We shall save each other," he murmurs before claiming my lips.

Desperate for the soothing balm of his caress to erase the nightmarish events of earlier, I reciprocate until nothing clouds my mind but sensation.

I awake alone and, for one blinding moment, I see Elize and Adair fragmenting into nothing behind my eyes. I sit up, forcing my eyes open. The room is dark, too dark, and panic smothers me. I scrabble from the bed, pushing the covers away, and go to the window. The heavy drapes reveal nothing and, disorientated, I am too terrified to push them back to see whether night has fallen once again.

Instead, I open my chamber door, make my way silently along the corridor and down the stairs. I encounter no one, and for one fraught moment, I imagine I am alone in the chateau, perhaps I ghost the building and a veil separates me from all others.

A thirst plagues me—not the sickness—but a true thirst and I push open a door to what appears to be a study in search of something to quench it.

I head for a sideboard holding an array of bottles. Reaching for a crystal decanter holding clear liquid, a sound alerts me to the fact that I am not alone. Turning, I see the duke lounging in an armchair next to the fire, a goblet hanging loosely from his long fingers. He is in a state of undress with his black shirt hung open to his navel, revealing a heavy, red-stoned pendant, and his feet are bare beneath his black trousers.

I startle and remove my hand from the decanter. He watches me with hooded gaze, before gesturing with his gobleted hand. "Please, allay your thirst... and join me."

I curtsy. "Thank you for the offer, Your Grace, but I shall leave you to your solitude."

"Oh, but I insist." Though he smiles, his tone is firm.

With a hand that shakes, I pour out a glass of water and lift it to my lips. I am vexed at finding myself alone with the duke, and for the fact that my fear is revealing itself in visible tremors.

"Come, daughter-in-law. Distract me from my melancholy."

I walk slowly over to the armchair opposite the duke and take a seat, setting the glass of water down on the table beside me. I am surprised the duke would indulge in melancholy. Surely that emotion is for one who has true feeling. Not a mockery of it.

He moves quickly, leaning forward to grasp one of my hands from my lap, and I bite back the squeak of alarm. "I am sorry one such as yourself had to witness that horrible sight, my dear. But let it serve as a warning to you."

"A w—warning?" I ask, hoping he will release me soon.

He smiles, white fangs gleaming in the firelight. "Indeed. Allowing your emotions to rule your actions has a way of ending in fire and destruction."

His hand caresses mine, and I fight the urge to pull it roughly from his grasp. I force myself to still, and lower my head.

"Without emotion what are we?" I murmur.

He tugs on my hand, pulling me to my feet, and looks up into my face. "So, so curious," he says, his eyes raking over me. "You are a mystery, my dear, and one I would take great delight in unravelling." His tone has lowered, and it sends disgust rippling out from my stomach in heavy waves.

"Ah, but she is not yours to unravel, Father." Lorcan's voice has me closing my eyes in relief.

I open them again to see the duke's amused gaze lingering on me before it shifts to over my shoulder.

"Perhaps not, Lorcan, but she *is* mine... in that *I* made her." The implication is clear. He made me, and so what I am belongs to him. Just as he pulled rank over Ines.

Lorcan comes up behind me, and finally the duke lets me go. I step back and press myself against Lorcan's chest. One hand snakes around my waist and anchors me to him. "Perhaps, that part of her," Lorcan concedes musingly, "but the part that truly matters... that is all mine."

I turn my head, so that I can look up into his face. He spares me one brief, fierce look, before resuming his dead-eyed stare of his father.

"Careful, my son, or else I may yet find you in flaming raptures in the courtyard. Do not forget, there is another who makes the same claim." The duke lets out a harsh, scornful laugh.

Lorcan stiffens against me. *Do not let him bait you*, I urge him in my mind. Lirrel has *no* such claim. Then he relaxes. "I am sorry to disappoint you, Father, but that is not what my future holds. Come, Roselle," he says.

The duke stares at us for one long moment, then waves an airy hand, dismissing us. Lorcan takes my arm and leads me away, but I feel the duke's gaze in the centre of my back like two flaming coals set there.

Outside in the foyer, Lorcan wastes no time in whirling to me. "*Why* were you alone with him? Do you seek danger?"

I take a step back at the low, harsh tone. "Of course not! I awoke alone, and I went in search of something to drink. I did not know he would be there."

Lorcan shakes his head as if frustrated at himself. "I'm sorry, Rose. Come, we should not speak so openly here." He once again takes my arm and escorts me up to our chambers, and into his room.

Once inside, I speak my mind. "Lorcan, please do not allow him to drive a wedge between us; he seeks to cause dissent with his acerbic comments. That is the true danger."

Lorcan takes a seat on the edge of his bed and, for one moment, I see such a vulnerable weariness there that I want to rush to him and soothe away his demons.

"It is not his comments that plague me, Roselle." He looks up at me, haunted pain clear in his gaze. "It is what's in here." He clutches at his head. "What I *imagine.*"

Now, I do go to him, but he stands and turns away before I even reach him. I feel the rejection as though he places a hand upon me and stayed my embrace. Horror curdles inside me. He imagines me with Lirrel. But how can he even think that I would give myself to any other? There is only him.

"*All* I am is yours, Lorcan," I tell his back huskily. "I hope one day you will hear the truth of it, and believe it." I walk over to the connecting door and let myself into my chamber and close the door behind me.

There is nothing else left to be said.

Chapter NINETEEN

"You are not eating, my dear. Is the veal not to your liking?"

Valentin leans towards me from his position at the head of the table. Disconcertingly, I was placed to his right, while Lorcan was seated further down and Yves at the other end of the exceptionally long table. Of Lirrel, thankfully, there is no sign.

"Oh, yes, it is beautifully cooked, Your Grace. I am just not hungry tonight," I say apologetically.

A flash of insight fills his gaze. He pats my hand in a fatherly gesture. "The loss of the Sorrences is felt by us all." I cannot help but flick a glance to Katerin, who sits opposite me. She gazes serenely back. Perhaps, I was mistaken in the identity of Adair's lover. The duc's emissary seems entirely unconcerned by the losses.

"I understand you enjoy reading. Perhaps you may permit me to show you the library here after we have concluded the meal? It may help to distract you," the duc continues and I turn back to him.

He does not fill me with the same dread as Duke Lamont, but I have no doubt as to the wealth of his power banked within his imposing figure.

Katerin gives me an encouraging smile. "It is the most opulent library you shall ever see."

The word 'opulent' triggers something in my mind, and I recall Elize talking about the opulence of the chateau when we first arrived, and then she had seen Katerin. Something unsettles me, as if two different conversations are taking place, and I do not understand the language of either. But visiting a library surely could not hurt?

I incline my head. "That sounds very agreeable. Thank you, Your Grace."

The duc smiles widely, just a hint of fangs showing, yet somehow I do not feel afraid. "*Parfait*. I shall look forward to escorting you and your husband."

Despite my lack of fear, knowing Lorcan shall be joining us settles something within me. Although, things are still hovering on a knife-edge between us, I hope Lirrel's continued absence will help, and surely a midnight excursion to a beautiful library can only lend a romantic setting to aid things along.

"And I, in turn, shall look forward to it too." I smile back prettily at the duc and he nods in approval.

I lean forward to pick up my wine glass, and feel a

gaze on the side of my face. I turn my head and see Duke Lamont staring at me from the other end of the table. I cannot tell if he is displeased. Surely, he wants me to be the effervescent daughter-in-law he mentioned at the picnic. Feeling brave, I lift my glass in a toast towards him, then take a sip.

As I lower the glass, I see his eyes have narrowed, yet I do not care. In this moment, I feel safe beneath Duc LaCroix's protection.

Ines' potion is still working and I feel better within myself than I have in an age. No painful burnings plague me, and no urges pull upon me. How long I can convince the duke of my strength in resisting what I should be seen as experiencing, I have no notion. But I will do all I can to prolong the charade. If Ines can do it, then so shall I.

If things were completely reconciled between Lorcan and I, I would ask if he wished to take the potion too. I tell myself he only drinks from animals, but in truth, I know not.

But I do know that it is going to take trust on both our parts to fully heal our rift.

I let my gaze wander down the table to covertly watch Lorcan as he converses with a lady from Duc LaCroix's court. Perhaps, he senses my gaze as he meets my eyes and I do not mistake the heat I see there.

My lips part at the memory of his touch.

"Ah, *l'amour*. Love transcends time, does it not?" Valentin murmurs and with a flush, I dip my eyes. Once again, I have allowed my emotions to reveal themselves for all to witness.

I allow a light laugh, brushing off the intensity of his statement. He has no idea that I will love Lorcan for a thousand centuries and it will never fade. "*Oui*," I respond. Just one word, but vast in its meaning.

The duc inclines his head, reaches for his glass and takes a drink, then stands. "My honoured guests, and members of my court, feel free to mingle. There is entertainment in the ballroom and of course the gardens." This time when he smiles, his full fangs are revealed and I caution myself to not forget who and what he is, however genial he acts towards me.

Dark laughter ripples around the table as the members of the combined courts push away from the table and filter away in groups or pairs. Sometimes, I can almost imagine we are simply in the dining room of one of the upper echelons of society and merely enjoying a sparkling dinner, but it is *these* moments that remind me, starkly, that we are not. The garments are just the wrong side of proper, and the conversation is not of who is getting married next, and what fortune they have… and the smiles, the smiles would *never* glint with fang and intent.

"Roselle?" Lorcan's voice pulls me from my spiralling thoughts.

"Ah, Lorcan. I have invited your lady wife for a tour of the library—she appeared a trifle out of sorts and I seek to elevate her spirits. I hope you will join us?" Duc LaCroix says.

Lorcan spears me a concerned glance, then nods. "Of course, I would like nothing more." He helps me stand, and tucks my hand into the crook of his arm.

"*Magnifique.* I shall meet you both there in just a moment." The duc smiles at us both.

Lorcan leads me out of the dining room, and takes me in the direction of a double-doored room opposite the ballroom. From a darkened alcove beside it, I feel avid eyes on me, and I repress the shudder. I know what awaits in the dark, but for a moment, I can pretend it isn't there.

We enter the room and, while we wait, Lorcan guides me along the rows of books, the tall shelves hiding us from view. "Have I told you how beautiful you look tonight?" he asks, stopping suddenly to trap me against the shelves.

A slow smile curves my lips. "I do not recall," I say, readily accepting the peace offering he extends following on from our last encounter. When his fraught imaginings drove a wedge between us.

"For shame, Cousin. How very remiss of you." If I hadn't been caressing Lorcan's face with my eyes, I would have missed the instant his features changed at the sound of the silky voice.

He is gone from me in an instant and the sound of two bodies connecting roughly against the bookshelves beside me is overlayed by a high-pitched gleeful laugh.

"I always did enjoy teasing you as a child, Lorcan. So glad I can still do so."

"Happy to oblige," Lorcan growls, and grips Lirrel tighter by the lapel of his pure-black high-necked shirt, thrusting him backwards against the shelves, which shakes the whole connected row.

"Lorcan—the duc!" I remind him, but he barely looks at me.

"I am more than happy to pay the price of any damages." He smiles slowly. "It will be so worth it."

Lirrel's eyes gleam with mirth. He is *enjoying* this. "Why do we not take this outside? Then the damage shall only be you... or... No, that's it, just you."

"Lirrel, stop it," I say in disgust, knowing now is not the time for retribution. "It is all over now. Do you think your uncle would approve of this behaviour in Duc LaCroix's court?"

Lirrel gives a one-shouldered shrug, but a glimmer

of something flickers in his eyes, and whatever mood had prompted this show vanishes. He shrugs out of Lorcan's grip as Duc LaCroix and Katerin turn the corner.

"What is all this?" the duc demands.

Lirrel straightens his shirt and sneers at Lorcan. "Nothing, Your Grace. Just a bit of fun between cousins."

Lorcan's face ripples with anger, while I step forward and lay a soothing hand on his arm.

The duc looks at Lorcan and I, and then at Lirrel. "Then I suggest it waits until another time. I have business with your cousin and his lovely wife."

Summarily dismissed, Lirrel tosses me a flashing grin, offers another sneer for Lorcan, and a bow for the duc. "Of course, forgive me." He slips away, and I rub Lorcan's tense arm. It does not soften beneath my touch, and once again, Lirrel has ruined everything.

"Lady Roselle?" The duc offers me his arm, and with no other option, I join his side and accept it. He leads me away from the shelves and over to the centre of the room. We stand on the tiled floor, and I see it is a mosaic of red, black, and silver roses intertwining and twisting all over the floor, thorny tendrils spearing out to each of the shelves that fan off like the numbers on a clock. "Look up," he invites, and I do with an exclamation of surprise.

It is domed like the foyer of the chateau, but stars glitter and gleam through the clear glass, not smoked like the glass in the foyer. The moon hangs heavy and full in the centre and I feel as though I am witnessing a portent of something magical.

"It is a Lover's Moon." Katerin comes up on my other side. "When love potions made beneath its pink glow work their best, ensorcelling all those who drink it." Her look is sly and for one moment, my doubts about her once again rear their head.

"Do not tease, Katerin," the duc admonishes. "Lady Roselle has no need for love potions. She weaves her own brand of magic... is that not so, Lorcan?"

Lorcan has silently joined us and I note he appears calmer as he stares up at the moon. "My wife has magic running through her veins, one that many would care to sup on," he says quietly, and my stomach clenches.

"Well, it is a good thing she is devoutly loyal to you, Lorcan," the duc's tone holds censure and both Lorcan and I look at him with surprise.

In the stunned silence, Katerin speaks up. "I was not speaking of Lady Roselle and Lord Lorcan, anyhow."

Valentin turns to her with a look of apparent warning, and Katerin releases her serene smile once again. The one she wore at the dinner table when we spoke of Elize and Adair. My eyes widen. Had she orchestrated their demise?

"Rest assured, my lady, my lord, the potion was only used on those *most* deserving of it."

"Katerin." This time there is no mistaking the warning.

She takes a step back and inclines her head respectfully at the duc, and I am puzzled by their dynamic.

"Shall we continue our tour?" The duc waves out an arm—dismissing the previous conversation—gesturing to the twin curved black metal staircases flanking the double-doors of the impressive library, and leading up onto another level.

I nod, and I am surprised when Lorcan takes my arm solicitously. Perhaps the duc's chastisement of him worked, and he is open to relinquishing me of any of the blame of Lirrel's hateful pursuit of me. Whatever it is, I welcome it. I smile up at him, and we follow Duc LaCroix and Katerin over to the left-hand staircase, climbing up to the next level. It wraps around the whole room, with more bookcases stacked to completion with tomes.

I cannot help but trail my fingers over each spine we walk past, wondering how many centuries it has taken to fill the shelves.

"You are welcome to borrow any of the books, you wish, Lady Roselle. But might I suggest you start with this one." Valentin stops at a bookcase, and removes a slim black leatherbound book. The spine is cracked and the gold gilt letters have been rubbed down to a dull sheen. He hands it over with one eyebrow raised, as if gauging my reaction. "When you have read it, I would be very keen to hear your thoughts."

I look down at the book. The title is in Latin. "*Ad Infinitum*," I murmur. "Forevermore."

The duc smiles, pleased. "You may be particularly interested in the last chapter... I certainly am."

I exchange a confused look with Lorcan, but I am intrigued none-the-less. "Thank you, Your Grace, I shall read it straightaway."

"*Bien*. Well, I shall wish you both a good night. Katerin?" The duc nods at us both, and I curtsy before he moves away.

"It is a really illuminating book," Katerin pauses to say, then glides away after the duc.

When they have both descended the stairs and moved towards the door, I look down at the book, and say, "I have no idea what just occurred."

Lorcan takes the book from me, and flips it open. "Neither do I, but I believe Valentin has a reason for wanting you to read it. Perhaps we should retire and see what it contains?"

The 'we' gives me hope. I want to discuss what happened with Lirrel, but that may trigger another chasm between us, so instead, I say, "That sounds like an excellent notion."

Lorcan slides the book into the inside pocket of his jacket and, once again, takes my arm.

We have barely descended the stairs when he is turning me into his arms and dipping his head, banked tension thrumming through him, as though the moment between us in the shelter of the book shelves had paused and we were now resuming it, brushing off the insolent interlude of Lirrel's interruption.

I am already straining to reach his lips as they move towards mine. I cling to him, revelling in his touch.

"If I never tell you that you are beautiful the moment my eyes alight upon you, you are fully within your rights to remind me, my wife," Lorcan says against my lips, and I smile in response.

"You do not have to say the words, I see it in your eyes," I say when we move apart.

"Dear, dear, what a vulgar display, children." Yves lounges against the doorframe of the open library doors.

To my surprise, Lorcan smiles. "Then, please, do let us remove ourselves from your sight, Father. Roselle, love, shall we continue this upstairs?"

With a flush staining my cheeks, and the duke's glower following us, Lorcan pulls me by the hand and hurries us away.

A giddy laugh erupts from me, as Lorcan spins me against the door to my chamber, and once again lowers his head to mine.

I forget about the book, and the strange interaction with Valentin LaCroix, as I lose myself in Lorcan and his suddenly teasing tactile administrations.

Chapter TWENTY

Lorcan trails a lazy hand over my bare shoulder, and a shiver of sensation ripples through me. "Can we just stay like this forevermore?" he drawls.

"Mmm-hmm," I reply, my mood tranquil, before the word filters through my sated mind and I sit up. "Forevermore. The book!" I scramble over him, and slide off the silky covers of the bed and pick up Lorcan's discarded jacket from the floor.

Lorcan watches me with amusement as I pull out the book from his pocket. "Well, that must be the first time I have ever been cast aside in favour of literature."

I spare him a smile, then crawl back into the bed and open the book. I scan the first few pages, and my tranquil feeling dissipates. The book contains dispassionate recollections and observations of immortal creatures, and how such things came to be. The book trembles in my hand; each detached recounting and study almost making a mockery of the suffering of so many. The many who did not choose this life, and had it thrust upon them.

"What is the matter?" Lorcan asks.

"It is abhorrent—the author did *experiments*. Why would Duc LaCroix think I would be interested in such a book?" I flinch away from the book as though it were a poisonous viper.

Lorcan picks it up thoughtfully. "He said the last chapter would be of interest, Rose," he reminds me gently, and thumbs through to the last section.

I lean back against the bedframe and close my eyes, suddenly so very, very tired. I do not know who to trust, which way to turn.

"Oh, darkness," Lorcan says in a tone that has my eyes shooting open. He is sitting up fully now, his eyes rapidly moving as he reads the text. Suddenly, his gaze is on me. "This is the answer." He turns the book around to show me.

"The answer to what?" I ask, as I reluctantly accept the book.

"To *everything*," Lorcan replies, and then he is out of the bed and dressing. "I must go and speak with Valentin. I suspect he has an ulterior motive in showing us that book."

I haven't even scanned the page. "Lorcan, I do not understand." I blink up at him.

He leans over and presses a hasty kiss to my lips.

"Read the chapter, I shall return." And he is gone.

I stare at the closed door for a few long moments before I lower my gaze and begin reading. The words start blurring together as I suddenly understand Lorcan's excitement as my own mounts…

It is curious that I should be so invested in the plights of these creatures, but I am. I find I have begun to feel pity for them, and endeavour to free them of their curse. Not merely by killing them. No, instead by the means of true liberty. And so, I turn my attentions not by how they were created, but how they could be—for want of a better word—un-created…

The book drops once again from my fingers, not through distaste, but instead from the trembling that wracks my hands. *True liberty… Un-created.* Had the author found a way? I hastily continue reading, and one line leaps out at me…

I have discovered that in order to return them to their mortal state—with all vestiges of the creatures they once were completely erased—the primary sire must be felled.

The sire.

Yves.

Nausea burns inside me. It is hopeless then. Duke Lamont is heavily protected, powerful. Lorcan and I would be executed if we even tried.

Despondency settling over me, I continue my reading.

I have discovered a network, a society of sorts, with each having a head. It is this head which must be removed in order to free all changed by them and their underlings. Merely killing any other than the head sire will have no effect, save for one less creature plaguing the land.

It must be Yves—only his removal will make a difference to us.

I set the book down. Why would Valentin wish me to read this? Was he toying with us?... *Here, here is the information you need, but you cannot utilise it in any way.* Lorcan's words come back to me. Does he believe Valentin wishes to *help* us? Why? Yves is his cousin, and centuries-old friend.

I push up off the bed. What if it is a trap? Fear cloaks me until I am scrabbling for my clothes and dressing swiftly. I tuck the book down the bodice of my gown and leave my chamber.

I hurry along the quiet corridors, not even knowing where I am going. Perhaps Ines will be able to direct me to Valentin. I head up the twisting tower stairs, knowing that is where Valdis and Ines have made their temporary accommodations.

I halt on the stairs as I hear steps coming down towards me. "Oh, my lady Roselle. May I assist you?"

It is Katerin. She smiles at me pleasantly.

I hesitate, not knowing if I can truly trust her,

despite her being Anaïs' daughter. She is emissary to the duc, after all. "I am looking for Duc LaCroix's quarters. My husband went to speak with him."

"Then I shall be happy to escort you," she says, her amber eyes bright.

She passes me on the stairs and I follow her down to the bottom and back into the hallway. I nibble on my lip, and hasten my steps to catch up with her dainty, yet, swift steps. She casts me a sideways glance, and I force a smile. An answering one twitches her lips. She is amused.

"You truly have nothing to fear from me, my lady. I wish no ill upon *you*—or your husband." There is that inflection again. Perhaps, she wishes Lorcan and I no harm, but there is someone she wishes it upon. I must know.

"Katerin. May I ask you something?"

"You may... but not here," she says, and then ushers me along another corridor and into a chamber. She waves her hand around us and I sense a stilling of the air. "You may speak freely now."

I stare at her for a moment, then with a nod, I say, "That love potion... who did you use it upon?"

She smiles widely, apparently pleased with my question. "I merely took advantage of a situation and removed two key adversaries. You should thank me, in truth."

"So you… you and Adair?"

Disgust flares in her eyes. "Once," she admits. "Before I knew him for what he truly was. He visited Paris with Duke Lamont, before he and Elize were together and, on one of his night-time prowls, we met. I fancied myself in love." Her tone and eyes are scornful. "My powers had not yet revealed themselves to me, but on the night of my eighteenth birthday they did… and that is not all that was revealed. I could *see*. See the true monster lurking beneath his handsome façade, and of Elize's when she came to warn me off the man she was intent on securing. My mother and Maxim arrived at, perhaps, a precipitous moment, and sent them scurrying on their way, claws sheathed. But Ines was not so lucky."

"Ines?"

Katerin nods, her amber eyes hazy with recollection.

"Yes, the next time Adair and Elize came to Paris, they were married, and high-up members of the duke's court. They were doing his bidding when he demanded they find one from my mother's coven. It didn't matter who, and so, Ines was the unlucky one. She did not even have time to protect herself. They swooped in and simultaneously attacked her, before leaving her for the duke to continue what they started."

Tears pool in my eyes as I think of my gentle friend. Ines' face morphs into Nisette's... into Coralie's... into my own. I blink away the visions.

"I was only too happy to take the role of emissary when my mother demanded a pact with Court LaCroix. She would not see another single member of our coven harmed." Now, Katerin smiles. "I have bided my time."

As I have mine.

"So, you encouraged Adair?"

"Hmm, surprisingly, he was hesitant to act on the lustful feelings he still held for me." Her lips twist as if the words taste bad on their way out. "So, yes, I slipped a little potion in his drink—which only enhanced what he already felt—and made sure Elize discovered us. I truly believed they loved each other, despite his desire for me. It was almost too easy."

I should feel disturbed, remembering what I witnessed of the Sorrences' miserable demise. But I find I cannot feel sorry, not now I have been privy to the whole story. "I am sorry for what happened to you, for what happened to Ines. Elize and Adair took great delight in carrying out the duke's orders with abundant glee." I step forward and take her hands in my own, and her eyes widen in surprise. "I am sorry I doubted you. Thank you," I say fervently.

She searches my eyes for a moment. "You have read the book?" I nod. "Then perhaps, now is the time for you to be a part of a wider venture." Intrigued, I wait, but she merely shakes her head. "I shall allow Valentin to explain. Come."

She waves her hand again, and the air clears. My thoughts are rioting as she leads me out of the chamber, along the hallway, and down the wide, curved staircase. We nod and smile at some court members who look to be at the end of a long night of revelry, both containing whatever it is we truly feel. I wonder how Katerin can stand to be around them all, knowing what she knows, seeing what she has seen. But then that is true for me too. Perhaps, we have learnt how to turn it off.

Beneath the staircase, we stop at a tall, arched, glossy black door, and Katerin knocks. Moments later, the duc pulls it open. He smiles as he sees us both.

"We were just discussing you, my dear," he says to me. "Please do join us." He pulls the door open wider to admit Katerin and I.

I step inside, relief filling me when I see Lorcan seated on a chaise longue the other side of a glowing fireplace in the opulent study. I hurry over to his side, and he reaches out a hand to take my outstretched one. He has an expression on his face I do not recognise. I look closer. It is optimism. I feel a smile beginning, one he reciprocates.

"Please be seated, Lady Roselle. We have much to discuss." The duc waves a magnanimous arm and I settle myself next to Lorcan, who rubs my hand soothingly. The duc sits in the armchair opposite and Katerin stands behind the chair, her usual serene expression back on her face.

I remove the book from my bodice, and hand it over.

"Thank you," Valentin says, a strange light in his eyes. "I trust you found it illuminating?"

I nod, but cautiously I say, "Very, but I still do not understand why you would share this knowledge with me—with us." I gesture to Lorcan.

The duc leans forward, and the glow from the firelight casts his face in sharp angles, and hooded planes. "Because, I sense you are not like us, my dear. You have no wish to embrace this life—ever. Am I wrong?"

My free hand flutters to my throat, as ghostly fangs prick my skin, and nightmarish memories batter my mind. I shake my head before I even realise it, and I am bestowed with three understanding gazes. It disconcerts me.

"Have no fear, I will not use this knowledge against you. *Au contraire*, I have a proposition for you both."

The last time a proposition was made by one such as the duc it did not bode well, but I am inclined that perhaps, this one will end in the reverse. Where Duke Lamont offered death—did Duc LaCroix offer life?

I look at Lorcan, and he says, "It does not hurt to listen to the duc, Rose."

"Of course," I say.

Valentin leans back, and crosses one leg elegantly over the other. "You are familiar with our Courts? How there are five?" Lorcan and I both nod. "Well, in the beginning there were four. One for each of the four siblings to head. The origins of our creation is quite tedious I am afraid—some would say we were cursed. However, I believe the opposite. I believe it is a gift. I, along with my two brothers and sister make up the four Courts. Europe, Americas, Russia, and Asia are their loose titles. But each court is vast and extends into the rest of the world too. It takes much organisation, as you could well imagine." The duc gives a tight smile. "In our folly, we decided to bring a descendent of our family—a distant cousin—into the fold and he *embraced* this life, far beyond what I imagined for us all. He convinced me to allow him control of Britain, leaving me free to concentrate on the mainland European Court." His gaze turns pensive, and I can only imagine just how ancient he and his siblings truly are, and just how many members number their Courts. The thought urges a shudder upon me, and I must fight hard to not release it.

"And it was folly indeed. His conduct, and those of his Court, threatens us all. He is rash, kills and turns indiscriminately. We have rules here at my Court, and the same is true of my siblings'. The courtiers you see here? They are here by choice. When it no longer becomes pleasurable for them, or they simply wish to leave, they are compelled to forget and leave with a pocketful of gold, with no ill will towards them. We *must* exist in harmony. There must be a balance. But Yves has forgotten that. What he did to you and your family, Roselle, is abhorrent beyond imagining."

"You—you know about that?" I whisper.

He uncrosses his legs, and leans across the gap to take my hand. "I know all there is to know."

I cannot look at Lorcan. If the duc knows of my family, then surely he must know of the impossible choice I made following their attack.

I see the answer in his ancient gaze. "Perhaps, what I propose to you now, will help towards more than just one's redemption."

I dip my head; shame and hope warring inside me.

The duc squeezes my hand. "Will you help,

Roselle? Help me reclaim the lost portion of my court?"

But his words are drowned out by the roaring in my head, the roar that calls for revenge. It is so close this time that I can almost taste it.

In doing this, I could secure that revenge... *and* free Lorcan and I.

I look up with a smile of my own.

"What must I do?"

Chapter TWENTY~ONE

Valentin exchanges a satisfied look with Katerin, and releases my hand. "Only my siblings and I can create a sire line, but when I allowed Yves his own court, I had a witch create a spell—she found a way to mirror the original enchantment we four are under, and thus he became a sire in his own right. His is contained to an amulet he always wears—but, and here is the problem, the amulet can *only* be removed by Yves of his own volition. You must find a way to induce him to remove it. Only then can I perform the rite needed to cleanse his complete sire line, and reabsorb them into my own, under one united court."

"His entire line?" Lorcan says thoughtfully.

The duc nods. "It is the only way. I must have complete obedience from my court members and the only way to ensure that is if they are under *my* sire line. They will be granted the gift of choice, just as you," he glances at Katerin, "and Ines, shall be. Become mortal, and go free, or stay and be welcomed into Court

LaCroix."

I jolt in my seat, unable to contain the leaping joy within me. "Oh, Lorcan, that means Ines shall be free, and Coralie too!"

His eyes are solemn. "And us, too, my love."

I clasp both his hands. Can this truly be happening? I do not think about *how* we are going to prompt the duke into removing his amulet, for now, I simply want to indulge in this moment of glorious, blessed hope. Not the faux hope that has tentatively sent out its seeking fingers, but true all-encompassing hope. There *is* a way out from this nightmare.

"I have one condition," Lorcan shocks me into saying and I search his face but he is wholly focused on Valentin.

"If I can but give it, it is yours," he replies, his eyes lit with intrigue.

"Lirrel shall never be granted immortality, he shall remain mortal. And I shall be permitted to deal with him as I see fit with no recriminations."

I slowly release my husband's hands, and he does not even look at me. Even now, as the light tries to glow in the dark, the spectre of Lirrel hovers over us, and hideous, sinuous suspicion rears its head in Lorcan's request.

Valentin flicks a look at me, perhaps noting my

statue-like demeanour, before nodding. "*Oui*. That is easy to agree to. Lirrel is much too like Yves for my tastes. In fact, I believe he over-indulged this night. He shall not bother you today." He spares a knowing smile at Katerin—and I wonder if she has yet again helped me by briefly incapacitating another of my foes—before he waves an imperious hand. "You shall avenge your wife's honour with impunity."

"It is not my *honour* to avenge, it goes far beyond that," I say quietly, and a rage flares up inside me. Surely, it should be I who gets to wield the means of justice to the one who betrayed me, and deceived me for a century.

Now Lorcan looks at me, and I stare steadily back. I have much to be ashamed of, but not what he believes occurred.

I turn away composedly and speak to the duc. "I will do whatever it takes to assist you, Your Grace. Katerin." I stand and smooth down the violet skirts of my gown.

The duc stands, followed by Lorcan. "It must be precipitous. Court Lamont removes itself back to England after the centennial ball tomorrow. I suggest you rest now as dawn fast approaches. I am sure a solution will present itself with clear minds. The duke is very taken with you, my dear. He will not suspect an ensnarement from you, I am sure, so you are perfectly placed to enact this." He gives me a telling look, and I immediately reject his words. The duke merely enjoys tormenting me.

"We shall find a solution, Duc LaCroix, I promise." I curtsy deep, and he helps me arise.

"I will await word from you both. Rest well." His smile includes Lorcan, beside me.

"Rest well," I repeat, and Katerin opens the door for us. I smile at her, and she gives me a kind one in return.

Silently, Lorcan and I ascend the staircase, and outside the door that leads directly to my chamber, I pause.

"Rest well, Lorcan," I say and slip into my room alone.

He does not even attempt to join me.

I awake from a restless sleep; my dreams had been filled with seeking fingers from shadowy figures and fangs flashing in candlelight, all while the duke's amulet swung like a pendulum in the background, each back-and-forth motion the droll chime of a death knell.

No sooner have I donned my robe than a knock comes at my door, and for one hopeful moment, I think it is from the connecting door, but it is not. I go to the outer door.

"Roselle? It is me, Ines."

I let her in quickly, and she slips inside. Her dark-blue eyes are wide when they look at me. "I have just spoken with Katerin. Is it true?"

I nod, and a genuine smile graces my face as hers blooms with the same hope that had filled me at the duc's speech.

"But we must discover a way to entice the duke to remove the amulet, or our hope is all for nought."

"Valdis explained to me the importance of the duke's amulet. He is keen for a new era," Ines says and I am surprised.

"Valdis too?" I recall the pity in his gaze as he helped the duke with the potion and the dark-magic-infused chain that bound me and Lorcan together. Perhaps, he too, is forced to do unspeakable things.

"Yes, he is old friends with Anaïs. He has been very good to me, protected me in every way he could. But he is bound to do Duke Lamont's bidding. I know not what the terms are, but he will be free of his bonds too, if we can find a way."

I steel myself. I must face my husband now.

"I shall get Lorcan. Perhaps, we three can produce a viable notion." I walk over to the connecting door and knock.

It is opened immediately, and Lorcan strides from within, his eyes intense on mine. For a moment, I hold his gaze, and I see the battle in the bright-blue depths. If only I can convince him that his fears are unfounded.

"Ines is here to help," I tell him quietly, and his gaze clears.

"Of course, time is of the essence." His tone is all that is formal and polite, and I wither a little inside.

We are on the cusp of freeing ourselves. What if we are free, yet the taunting demons of torment do not leave his mind? What then? Once I had believed I was strong enough to let him go. If his forgiveness I could not win, then I would remove myself from his existence. But now? Now, I cannot bear to even contemplate ever letting him go.

We are bound, not by the silver chain of enchantment, but by the shining thread of love. I pray to whatever god will hear me, that I will get a chance to prove it to him. That I have never been unfaithful. Faithless, yes, but *never* unfaithful.

"Lord Lorcan, you know the duke best. Do you have any ideas on how to persuade him to remove the amulet?" Ines asks. "How about when he is resting or bathing? Would he remove it then?"

"He always has guards protecting him at his most

vulnerable moments," Lorcan replies. His eyes turn thoughtful, and then they rest heavily on me. "I can think of one instance where he will not be guarded and his own guard would be lowered in turn."

I do not like the way he is looking at me. I fear he is about to suggest something entirely abhorrent.

"Then what is it?" Ines asks. "We must act swiftly."

"Roselle—" Lorcan begins, and I immediately shake my head.

"No," I whisper, suddenly knowing exactly what it is he is about to request of me. Can I sink even lower than the pit of hell I currently reside in? "No, Lorcan, you cannot ask this of me."

"Valentin was correct. He would not suspect sabotage from you. He desires you, Roselle… it is the only way." Lorcan moves closer and I see Ines' eyes widen in shock over his shoulder.

This a test. A way to prove my loyalty, surely? Shards of ice penetrate deep. "No, I will not betray you this way, Lorcan. I have *never* betrayed you this way," I add pointedly, and his expression turns stony. "We will find another option." My voice is firm, despite the tremors rippling beneath my skin. But it is more than that; my very essence crawls.

Lorcan suddenly cups my cheek, despite Ines' presence, startling me. "You will only have to pretend,

Rose, just long enough to make him think you are willing."

"He will know it for a ruse, Lorcan." I lean into his hand, and add in a whisper, "He knows how I feel about you."

Lorcan's eyes flare briefly, then the shield returns. "Not if we orchestrate a little scene of our own and, heartbroken, you turn to him, seeking solace."

"Solace? From… from *him*? Lorcan, he stole every single one of our lives from us! How can you possibly ask this of me? How can I possibly hide the depth of my hatred for him?" Distaste licks through me; a sulphurous wave. "And he is… he is your *father*…"

Lorcan releases my face and a strange expression crosses his face. "He is not my father," he says in a dead tone, eyes slicking with a reddened sheen. "He married my mother when I was a young boy and when the time was right he turned me into this, moulded me in his image, and cast her aside to die." I stare at him in horror. I thought I knew true hatred of the duke, but it is nothing to what Lorcan has been concealing all this time. "If *I* can hide it, you can too for just one night."

I take a step back. "Oh, Lorcan, I had no idea," I say gently, and Ines retreats further away, giving us the illusion of privacy, although she will still hear every word.

"Few do. The duke prefers it that way," Lorcan says, the red receding as a weariness enters his tone. "We look enough alike that none question my true origins."

Slowly, I find myself nodding, though my body revolts at the thought of carrying out the wicked charade. How far will it take me? To the edge of the abyss and beyond. "Very well, I shall do it. If it means ending this nightmare then what is one more sacrifice?" My voice does not sound like my own.

"I am *truly* sorry that I ask this of you," Lorcan says, his voice hoarse, and our eyes lock.

Ines speaks up. "I will do all I can to assist you, Lady Rose. A potion should dull his senses enough that he is not wholly aware of your intent, but you will need to get close enough to administer it." Her eyes are filled with pain, and I see that it is the pain of awareness. She too was thrust into a situation wholly unwanted with a creature who did unspeakable things to us all.

"I understand," I say, and try to swallow, but my throat is coated with invisible fangs, as if each one seeks to cut off any further acquiescence from me.

Lorcan dips his head as if in shame, and turns away. "I shall meet with you both later. I must go and speak with Valentin and set the stage for your perceived heartbreak, Roselle."

I follow him to the door, and place a hand on his arm, and for one moment, I think he may not acknowledge it, but at the last moment, he takes my hand in both of his and looks down at me, the battle back in his eyes. I see now what this request of me is costing him. He believes I was wanton in his absence, and now he actively demands it of me... because there is no other alternative. Oh, how the dark deities must be laughing up at us now. "Whatever you witness later, you must react as if it is real, as though it cuts you to the quick."

"Lorcan, what?..."

He shakes his head. "In order for this all to work, for us to finally be free, it must be deemed as real, my love. Do you understand?"

"I understand," I say dully for the second time. Even his use of the endearment only causes a brief flicker of warmth within my frost-covered body. I have no other choice but to understand. This path we tread upon grows more precarious by the second, and like quicksand, it can pull us all ruthlessly under before we even realise what is occurring.

Lorcan searches my face for one long moment, then he swoops down and captures my lips. "This is what is truly real," he murmurs against my skin, then he is gone, pulling the door open and striding through it.

Mutely, I watch him go, my fingers pressing against my lips as if I can keep his kiss there for eternity, until Ines joins me and settles a comforting hand upon my shoulder.

"You shall endure it," she tells me softly. "You are stronger than you realise." But I believe it is Ines who is the strong one. I can only imagine what horrors she has witnessed being sequestered in the duke's court for a century.

I turn to her with a sad smile. "I must endure it, so that we may all be free," I say, and she inclines her head.

"I wish for nothing more," she replies.

"Then shall we prepare?"

She nods. "Indeed. I will leave you to dress, and go and create the potion I spoke of."

"I await your return."

She gives me a smile before gliding out of my chamber. I close and lock the door behind her. Only then do I stumble to the bed and allow my head to fall into my hands, releasing the tears that I have kept at bay.

I should have none left to cry. I should be hollowed out, but yet I still retain the essence of fear and grief.

But one more act it will take of me, to finally

release my shackles.

One final clash; the deadliest yet, but my weapons shall be seduction and ingénue. I only hope they shall be enough against centuries-sharpened teeth, and an even sharper mind.

I dread I may not win this time.

But yet, I must try.

Chapter TWENTY~TWO

I dress with intent, in a gown of pale pink but, with one swish of the skirts as it catches the light, it gleams red. The low cut reveals my bare shoulders and slender neck, while the bodice glitters with hundreds of tiny iridescent red and clear gemstones. A confection of organza, gauzy net, and lace come together to create a voluminous skirt. It is like nothing I have ever worn before, in this incarnation or the last, and it is certainly something none in the duke's court has witnessed adorning me.

My hair, I pull up on top of my crown in a mass of curling ringlets and anchor with faux roses in a deeper shade of red-pink. As a final touch I secure a heavy blood-red ruby around my neck on a pink velvet ribbon.

In the mirror I see an illusion. Of a girl with pale cheeks, overlarge eyes, and crimson lips, dressed to tease and entice with alluring innocence. But it is in sharp contrast to what churns beneath. Horror, caged

horror, shall dictate my every move, all while a seductive smile graces my lips.

I slip red beaded heels onto my feet, and stand.

A knock comes at the door and I hasten over to it and admit Ines. She slips inside quickly and scans my appearance with a heavy expression. "I am sorry," she says and I know she understands how much this is taking from me.

"It is a necessary evil," I reply.

She nods, then holds out a small glass jar. "I am sorry for this as well, but you must... smear it over your lips. It must touch his skin, and that is the only way to ensure it happens."

My eyes widen at what she is implying, and nausea roils through me in heavy suffocating waves. No. I thought I could do this but I cannot. *I cannot.* I press a hand to my stomach as all within me revolts.

"Lady Rose. It is the only way," Ines says, her firm, yet sympathetic, tone breaking through my panic.

I blink at her, and slowly remove my hand from my stomach to instead hold it out to her and accept the jar. It was inevitable, of course, the moment I agreed to this madness, that fate would mock me and force me into this shadowy world of dark seduction.

I return to my dressing table and uncork the jar. A subtle scent of roses—how very appropriate—assails my nostrils and I look at the glistening red creamy substance.

"It will blend in with your lip colour," Ines tells me. "It is perfectly safe for you as I mixed one drop of your blood into the ingredients. It will only affect whomever you kiss—so have a care to refrain from seeking out your husband. We need him focused for this."

I dip my head, avoiding her gaze in the mirror, feeling the heat staining my cheeks. I select a tiny brush from those on my dressing table and dip it into the cream. "What will it do?" I ask as I lift the brush and inspect the red droplet on the bristles.

"Intoxicate him... he will feel as though he has over-indulged. He will become sated and clumsy. Easy for you to entice him into removing the amulet."

I hesitate then slick the substance over my lips, until they gleam and glisten like two ripe cherries. My lips tingle, but not uncomfortably. "How long do I have?"

"For as long until you wipe it away," Ines says. "Come, I will escort you to the ballroom. Lord Lorcan sent word that he wishes you to meet him there. The ball has just begun."

I stand and smooth down my skirts, every nerve-ending standing to attention; the spectacle is about to begin, and we will all have to play our parts—however disturbing.

"Very well," I say, and together we leave my chamber. I feel detached, as though what I am is slowly slipping away, tethered only by one single shining thread of hope. Hope that we will be victorious.

We walk along the silent corridors, and down the sweeping marble staircase as ghost-like staff flit around the entry foyer. We continue on until we reach the ballroom, and Ines melts away to leave me framed within the open doorway. The raucous sounds die down as all eyes turn my way. Well, I certainly desired to make an entrance, and it seems I have secured that desire.

I scan the room before I walk in, wondering if Ines will follow or if her role in all this is now complete. I see now I was correct in my choice of gown. I stand out. All others are dressed in the favoured darker attire, and it takes me a moment to locate my husband. When I do, I feel as though I have died all over again. But this time it is with a dagger to the heart, and not merely a bite to the neck.

Lorcan reclines lazily in a long low seat next to Duc LaCroix and Yves, all three cradling young ladies on their laps in various states of adoring compulsion, while others hover around them, perhaps awaiting their turn. My eyes track the blood trailing down the neck of the woman on my husband's lap as it vanishes beneath the lowered bodice of her gown. Nausea; thick and dark enclaves me, filling me like oily tar yet I force myself to meet his eyes, allowing the full extent of the betrayed hurt I feel deep within to show in my gaze. Is this how he felt when he believed I had draped myself over Lirrel and allowed him to sup his dark desires?

Oh, darkness, if he felt but half of what I am now feeling then how did he bear it?

Coarse laughter ripples around the room, and the scene recommences around me with court members continuing in their own dance of depravity.

I feel my head whirling as Valentin LaCroix's expression changes to one of banked triumph; he knows our plan, but it is Lorcan who my attention fixates on. He lowers his head, eyes on me—and for a moment I see the desire he feels for me in his gaze—before he trails a kiss along the woman's neck. *It is not real, it is not real*, I chant in my head, but what I *feel* is real. So painfully real. But I have a role to play in all this too. And I shall do it well, using the wounds inflicted to fuel me.

I allow a sound of pain to emit from my lips, one hand fluttering to my breast, and tears to pool into my eyes before I cast an anguished look at Duke Lamont.

His eyes flicker with crimson heat at my obvious distress—predator toying with prey—before he lowers his gaze taking in my revealing gown. Lorcan was right; the duke does desire me.

I let my gaze linger on his, widening my tear-pooled eyes slightly, then I whirl about and rush from the room, instinctively knowing he will follow me as though compelled.

I slow my steps, leaving my scent like breadcrumbs, as I head for the duc's vast gardens. I aim for the rose-covered bower and settle onto the curved bench, framing myself perfectly.

I do not even have time to spare a glance upwards and soothe myself with the stars before I sense a movement before me.

Yves, flanked by two of his guards; Draven and Keir, stares hungrily down at me.

My first act is to dispense of the guards, so I open my eyes wide and effect a sob. "How could he betray me like that after I *waited* for him?" I manage, holding one hand out to him imploringly. "For a century!"

"Leave us," the duke says and while the guards hesitate, he spears them with a glare. Immediately, they melt away and head back towards the chateau.

I hide my nervous swallow as the duke takes a seat close beside me. "Oh, my dear Roselle. You still do not understand our ways do you?" he says, and I am surprised to hear genuine sympathy in his tone. "I know you fight it still, but if you would only partake you would be free to join us all, and see the liberty it affords you. You can be whoever you want, be *with* whoever you want."

I only want my husband, I think desperately, but still I turn doe-eyes his way. "Would it make this pain stop?" I ask him in soft anguish.

His eyes flare red. "I could make it stop," he says, his voice lowering, and one hand snakes out to caress my cheek. Perhaps he sees Elize's desperation in me, and seeks to truly assuage my pain… but no, of course not; he is greedy and self-absorbed, and would only do this to enhance his own base pleasure. I close my eyes. The power ripples through him; I sense it in his touch. If I was but still a mere mortal, I would be completely and utterly at his mercy.

But as it is, *I* hold the power. He is ripe, and all I need to do is pluck him. Just one taste is all it will take. My lips part and I sense his gaze sharpen, his fangs lengthen.

I open my eyes, and lean infinitesimally into his hand. "Make it stop," I whisper. "*Please.*"

I fully comprehend my own power when the duke seems to shudder, the planes and angles of his face turning sharper, honing themselves into something primeval, before he takes both my upper arms into his hands, pulling me close.

I wait for *the* moment, but instead he releases me. "No, this requires privacy," he says, more to himself, and I am surprised, but a thrill of fear runs through me. Outside, I can still flee if need be but sequestered in his chamber?

I do not have time to ponder my predicament before the duke takes one hand and whirls me away. I blink and we are outside the double-doors to his bed chamber.

I briefly note the absence of his guards before he leads me into his room and closes the doors behind us. I force myself to give a coy smile. I have opened Pandora's box, all that remains is to unleash what lies within.

"Unpin your hair," the duke commands huskily, and my eyes widen.

Slowly, I do as he bids, removing each faux rose and dropping them to the pale carpet so they lay scattered around me; bloodstains on the snow. My hair falls in an abundance of curls and waves and I see true desire ripple across Yves' face... but then he smiles; sharp and bright. How foolish of me. I made the mistake of confusing him with a mere man. He is a *monster.*

I am rewarded with my obedience by a horrifying flashback to my turning when the duke is suddenly upon me, and backing me over to his wide, canopied bed.

His earlier sympathetic tone vanishes, replaced with dark triumph. "Oh, how I have longed for another taste of you, Roselle." He lowers me to the cushions and every fibre of my being screams at me to *run*. "That moment of your turning was not enough. Do you know how I have craved you ever since that moment? Why do you think I had Lirrel remove you from my sight… the temptation would have proved too much. I knew I had to punish you and Lorcan for going against my will, but really how could I blame him? Beauty is always temptation. Simply the scent of you is too intoxicating. So very, very intoxicating…" His eyes ravage me, until I feel it like painful incisions on my frozen skin. "But now, you have come to me. You should have always sought *me*. My son cannot compare."

I steel myself, knowing that this is the moment I truly turn to the monster inside. I arch upwards, instigating the duke's claim. "Yes, my duke," I murmur and he makes a growl of appreciation. But he does not know. I am the puppeteer this time, and yet I will sacrifice myself on the altar of freedom. Whatever it takes. If I am damned, I shall damn him too.

All it takes is one kiss.

One brief melding of flesh.

But *I* shall be the one who deems where it falls. I skim his face with one small hand, before tilting his head away, and I see the intrigue in his gaze as I lean in to his neck. Oh, the exquisite irony, I think. A bite for a bite.

I press my infused lips to his skin next to where the throbbing of his pulse should be, and I imagine, as my lips linger, that I am truly halting its progress... as he did with mine. And for one thrilling moment, it is I who is intoxicated at the sheer feminine power I now wield.

"That feels so good," the duke says, his voice thickening and slurring. *It is working, thank darkness.*

"Mmm-hmm," I murmur, and toy with the collar of his shirt, pulling open the ties to reveal his pale skin—and the red-black amulet nestled amongst his dark chest hair. "What is this?" I ask, my voice a purr. I trail one finger around the amulet.

I am no longer afraid. Now, he is in *my* thrall.

The duke leans back languidly against the cushions. "That interests you, does it?" he asks thickly, a small smile playing around his lips, while his eyes appear hazy.

I lean over him. "Everything about you interests me, my duke," I simper. It will soon all be over. Soon. *Please darkness.* "May I have a closer look?" I look up him from beneath my lashes, and his eyes fixate on my lips.

He must be the one to remove it, I remind myself. Only then will the protection be revoked.

Even in his subdued state, I sense the hesitation in him, so I once again lower my lips to his skin right next to the amulet. It leaves a sticky red imprint there—a scarlet brand of my betrayal—and he bucks beneath me, one hand clamping my loose hair.

"Please," I murmur.

This time there is no hesitation. He releases my hair, and I straighten to watch him snake his hands around the back of his neck to undo the amulet.

Patience.

He holds it out and I open my palm. If I had breath to hold, I would have held it back as the instrument of my freedom—of so many others' freedom—hangs suspended between us, like a guillotine waiting to drop. Our eyes meet as it falls into my hand and I cannot help but show my true delight, as I cup it to me.

Finally.

His eyes darken through the haze. He knows

something is not right. Now is the time to retreat.

I slide from the bed, taking the amulet with me, and he struggles to sit up. As I stare at him from halfway across the room, for one heady moment, I imagine doing it. Doing it myself. Taking his life—or whatever name this unholy existence calls itself—as he had stolen mine.

Revenge will be mine. Vengeance is my name.

A rage comes over me, unlike any other I have experienced before. It is red and cloying, slicking over my vision like a veil, and before I fully comprehend what I am capable of, I am already smashing a chair to the floor, so the legs splinter off in satisfying ready-made wooden stakes.

I blink and one is in my other hand, and I am advancing on the bed.

"Roselle. What are you doing? *What have you done to me*?" The last words come out in a roar, which seems to shake the very foundations of the chateau, as the duke's ancient beast tries to battle past the potion.

I raise the wooden stake high, unable to control my actions. I will no longer be used and abused and a plaything of this court.

I release myself.

Chapter
TWENTY~THREE

Yves twists away but his movements are still slow and ungainly and he slips backwards onto his elbows. The stake arcs down, and I watch it in a detached way, but at the very last moment, my hand is caught in a firm grip.

"*No*, Roselle. No, it must be Duc LaCroix." Lorcan pulls the stake from my grip and tosses it away.

My retribution is torn from me and with a cry, mourning every pain, every loss, I crumple to the ground, the amulet clutched against my chest. I rock back and forth, soundless sobs erupting from me.

I know it must be Valentin who carries out the deed, but still I want it. Crave it. When will *I* get to punish those who have wronged us all? I feel as though I am splintering apart in my devastation.

But sometimes things must be broken for them to be fixed.

I have to break so that which resides within me could be freed. Free to fulfil its purpose. And now I see what that purpose is. How fitting that the creator should be felled by its own creation. The loop closes, the sands of time sigh out its last breath... a long drawn out hush. Silencing the era of Yves for good. It doesn't need to be by *my* hand; I am the spark, Valentin LaCroix will be the flame of retribution.

I collect the scattered pieces of me, and gather them into my soul. Re-building fragment by tiny fragment, limning the seams with iridescent gold akin to the Japanese art of kintsugi. What was once broken, can be better than it was before. Superior in its flaws. I shall wear my scars with honour, but they shall only be visible to me. Each one a network of paths leading me back to redemption. To, hopefully, forgiveness. Infinitesimal veins knitting back together at the severance points. Those points only recognisable by me. Soothed into healing by me. When Lorcan lifts me gently into his arms, I know he will be my healer too.

I am vaguely aware of movement around me from others in the room. "You did it, Rose. You did what was needed to secure our freedom. It is all right now," Lorcan murmurs into my hair. But I know it is not over yet.

Yves roars again and I look over Lorcan's shoulder to see Duc LaCroix's guards, headed by Katerin, securing the duke in a silver chain. Valdis and Ines observe with dispassionate eyes.

Bile rises in my throat at the sight of the chain, and the memory it evokes.

"Do not look at him, my love," Lorcan urges.

But I cannot drag my gaze away as the duke is escorted past me, accusing blood-red gaze devouring me, and I know I shall see that image in my nightmares for the rest of my existence. That will be my penance... and my reward.

He makes a sudden movement and turns, straining at the chain, and a lick of fear spectres my spine. "I could have made you a queen," he hisses at me, "but all you shall be now is fodder for the worms."

Lorcan growls, but I rest a hand on his shoulder. "And you shall be nothing but dust and an odious memory," I reply, satisfied that my voice does not shake, though every part of my body trembles.

The duke sneers, but Katerin appears surprised and impressed by my retort, and bows her head in a deferential manner to me before making a gesture to the guards with her hand. The guards yank on the chain and Yves is pulled from the room. Valdis inclines his head at me as he follows, but Ines approaches Lorcan and I. She accepts the amulet when I hand it over.

"Thank you, Roselle, you have freed us all," she whispers and the trembling in me subsides.

"I could not have done so without you," I murmur back, and she gives me a small smile, before she follows after Valdis and the others.

In the aftermath, Lorcan lowers to the floor, with me cradled in his lap. He buries his face in my hair, and we just cling to each for one long moment.

The stench of betrayal should linger over us, but it does not for silently we say our apologies. Both of us had done what needed to be done. Both of us maintaining a persona that was not *us*. Other characters took our places and we watched as though observers from within. I know this now.

Lorcan lifts his head and takes my face in his hands, his intent clear. Perhaps he wishes to erase the abhorrent taste of all else from me.

"No, do not kiss me, Lorcan. You shall become intoxicated."

"Oh, Roselle, I already am." His eyes soften. "I already am." His forehead drops to mine.

The first stirrings of a genuine smile grace my lips. "As I am by you," I whisper.

"Come, we must bear witness to Duc LaCroix's reabsorption of Yves' court." Lorcan lifts me off him and helps me stand, before rising himself.

I nod. Though the rage has left me, I still need to see the duke's demise with my own eyes. I need to see justice served.

Despising the dress I wear, I reach down and have no qualms in ripping a strip from the hem to use to rid my lips of Ines' potion. I scrub and scrub until my lips throb. Would that I could remove the top coating of skin and expunge the memory of the last flesh it touched. I withdraw the fabric to see the shimmery pink-red organza smeared with scarlet.

Red upon red upon red.

Layers of it scourge my mind, yet it is somehow grounding. I have become numb to the sight over the years, but I vow, I shall never wear red again.

"Now I am going to kiss you," Lorcan states, and takes me in his arms. Heat pools low and deep in my stomach as his lips meet my now naked ones. I kiss him back as though drawing life-giving breath from him, though I need it not yet, and pull him flush against me by his jacket lapels.

We break apart, eyes heavy and sated on each other.

"This is only the beginning," Lorcan promises and takes my hand.

Now that is one promise I can believe.

He leads me from the room, and I notice how deathly silent it is. We meet no other members of the court or staff until we enter the ballroom, and the scene is one far removed from the debauchery of an hour ago. No compelled courtiers or sycophantic sympathisers are to be seen, only the members of both Court Lamont and Court LaCroix are congregated before the dais. Upon which stands Duc LaCroix, Valdis, Ines, and Katerin next to a restrained, savage-faced Duke Lamont.

"There are the traitors," the duke snarls and all eyes turn to Lorcan and I as we walk through the aisle cleaving the two courts.

"*Au contraire*, Yves, they are no traitors. They were doing as I bade them. This is *my* court, and I am to be obeyed." Duc LaCroix's eyes pierce Duke Lamont's. "You did not heed my warnings, Cousin. I have been far too lenient with you, but no more. This ends tonight."

Murmurs ripple through the crowd and nervous looks pass over the faces of Duke Lamont's court.

Lorcan and I position ourselves next to the dais, and a gentle breeze floats in from the open terrace doors behind me, bringing with it the scent of frost and rose.

I step back, allowing the light wind to ripple over me. I need the sensation of something external to keep me from focusing on what is happening within me. The sudden hope is unbearable.

I try to concentrate on Duc LaCroix's speech. "When I reclaim Court Lamont, all those personally changed by Yves Lamont, and those by them in turn, will be returned to their mortal state."

Angry shouts erupt from Duke Lamont's court, while the duke's face turns to one of hunted terror. I push away any sympathy at the sight. *He is a monster*, I remind myself, and deserves no pity.

Duc LaCroix holds up one hand, and silence falls instantly.

"All those who wish to remain thus, are free to leave with my protection." His gaze slides over Lorcan and I, and the hope morphs into something with wings. I fear my still heart will simply float away from me before it has even had the chance to yield its first beat. "All others who wish otherwise shall be changed and welcomed into the new Court."

The murmurs start again as Duke Lamont's court turn to each other, eyes speculative. I wonder how many will choose as Lorcan and I have. How many will be capable of living a mortal life, knowing what they have done to other mortals in pursuit of immortality and depravity. But surely, even continual pleasure-seeking wears thin after a while?

"I will allow a little time for what is left of Court Lamont to make their decisions." Duc LaCroix removes a silver stake from a box on the podium on the dais, and I watch the light spear off it, highlighting Duke Lamont's face in brutal jagged blades.

Resigned to his fate, Yves tilts his head up and looks scornfully at his court before he bestows a violent look on me. I can see his thoughts. I bested him, and he regrets not disposing of me when he had the opportunity.

I allow a small victorious smile to grace my lips before taking another step back, my hand seeking a wall to lean against. I am suddenly weary; the fight in me stilling. But all I feel is gossamer curtains, blown against my hand.

I stiffen; every instinct in me sensing danger. I open my mouth to alert Lorcan but it is too late. A slender-fingered hand clamps over my mouth and unseen by anyone else—all distracted with what is occurring on the dais—I am whirled away and into the gardens.

Horror curdles inside me and I do not even need the gift of sight to know who my assailant is.

I am already running the moment I am released. Lirrel's silky laugh follows me. I head for the hedge maze, seeking only to lose myself until Duc LaCroix carries out his justice. Only then will Lirrel no longer be able to track me with his centuries-honed skills.

"Oh, my lady," Lirrel croons, from behind me… no… to the right. Disconcerted, I make a turn and keep going, clutching the skirts of my gown in my hands as I seek escape.

I make another turn and with horror, I see I have double-backed on myself and run straight out of the maze and nearly into Lirrel's arms.

"*No*," I say, as he laughs, and stumble away, but he is quick. Had always been quicker, and his arms are banded around me already. *Lorcan!* I cry in my mind, my heart shattering. If we are released from our immortality now, Lirrel could take me far away in the commotion, to a place where Lorcan would be unable to track me, no longer having his supernatural gifts.

Lirrel is unkempt and his gaze wild. "I have you now," he murmurs, taking in one long inhale of my hair, and I struggle. But he appears to enjoy that, so I cease and hang limply in his hold as he whirls us away into the courtyard, and roves his feral gaze over my face. He lifts his head, as if scenting something, then a slow smile works its way across his features. "Oh, this is going to be diverting," he continues gleefully and, with surprise, I find I am free.

"Roselle!" Lorcan's shout reaches my ears. "Why did you leave?" His eyes search me in confusion as he joins me in the centre of the courtyard. "It is all going to be well now, the duc is about to do the deed."

"No, no, you don't understand," I ramble, but he takes me in hold, trying to soothe me. "We must go now!" But a terror, so complete, so all-encompassing fills me as he stiffens in my arms, and I see over his shoulder Lirrel grinning a wide crazy smile as Lorcan jerks.

"Oh, no, no, no," I say, hands pressing over my still—yet still broken—heart, knowing what is happening. The scene before me is mirroring what is about to happen within the ballroom.

I cannot bear it. I cannot stay and watch my husband's demise. Call me a coward but as Lirrel pulls his arm back, I stagger away to stumble through the stone archway. I cannot watch him turn to dust. All our hopes and dreams turn to dust. Potent fragrance assails me to the point of suffocation, as the thorns on the black rose bush catch at my skirts. I gag, everything within me revolting, as a possessive hand lands upon my shoulder.

Lirrel has apparently not wasted any time in lording over his victory, and follows me; his true undertaking. I whirl to him in a sudden fury, fingers seeking to rake down his face, to spit and claw and kick, but he overpowers me. Even in my wrath, he is stronger than me. He grabs at me painfully, but I trip over the stone bordering the path and I fall, pulling from his hold.

I crumple sideways to the ground, my head cushioned by my mass of curls, but still the impact jars through me, rippling out into spider-webbed fractures. Frozen, I can only stare at the stained glass window of the small building in my eyeline. All sound filters away and I am caught between time and space, neither here, nor away. Captured in this suspended moment. Lorcan is gone.

Gone, gone, gone.

Gone where I cannot follow. My mind shatters and I fear—no, I *hope*—that I will lose myself to madness.

The light plays with the coloured glass and through my tear-filled eyes, the images seem to shift and whirl. Colours blending and spinning and instead of madness becoming my sanctuary, I am thrust back into a memory. One that I had long forgotten but now, perhaps released by the impact, has been loosened within my mind…

…"Here, my lady." A long cylindrical golden device is placed into my hand.

I look up at Lirrel. "What is it?"

"Set it against your eye," he says with a smile.

I indulge him. With the backdrop of the night-time

Frost Fayre behind him, I place the device against my right eye. The other end of the device is filled with coloured glass fragments. Lirrel turns the end and, I cannot help the exclamation of surprise that leaves my lips, when the fragments move and create a new pattern. He turns it again and a star shape appears before my eye.

"So beautiful," I murmur, and for this one moment, this one crystalline second, I am content; happy almost. Everything fades away as I take in the surprising beauty that can still be found in this cold, cruel existence.

I look at Lirrel, at the tiny snowflakes powdering his loose blonde hair, at his eyes intent on mine, almost a caress. "Thank you," I tell my friend and offer him the device back.

His gloved hand covers my own and he says, "It is a gift for you."

"You are too good to me," I reply, but I am pleased with the gift. I stow it inside the deep pocket of my dark purple cloak.

He dips his head for a long moment before he lifts it and offers me his arm. "Shall we?"

My happy feeling dissipates. For a moment I caught a flash in his eyes, a glimmer of something ancient and cold... and so predatory and possessive that

I am loath to take his arm, but I force myself to shake off my unease. Lirrel is my friend, my sole companion. I must allow that the demon in us all sometimes reveals itself.

I lay my small hand on his arm and he leads me away from the frozen lake and back towards the striped tents of the fayre set beneath the clear star-pocked sky. The scent of frost mingles with cinnamon spice and tempting chocolate, and I resume my normal emotive state. Serene in my outward appearance yet simmering just beneath with disquiet.

A child's yell of joy reaches my ears as a young boy barrels past, holding aloft a red, yellow, and blue ribbon streamer…

Chapter
TWENTY~FOUR

I blink away the clouds of the memory, and I am forced brutally back into the present; the stained glass window's bright colours still within my eyeline.

Tears obscure my vision and the glass seams to crack. Is that all I am ever to experience; a kaleidoscope of beautiful chaos? One wrong move, one pivot, and the scene changes. Stars and diamonds shining brightly, but one jolt and they dissolve, replaced by something as sharp and jagged but without clear form. Without purpose. Just like me. What am I now?

I try to crawl away, gravel piercing my skin through the filmy garment of my skirts, and pressing into the palms of my hands, but I welcome the pain. Use it to feed my hunger to evade my captor. I crawl like an animal, no humanity left within me. Erased by that one violent act mere moments ago. How ironic that, in the moment of my mortality soon to be granted back to me, all I have left is animal instinct—*prey always flees predator*—and indistinct babbling, sobbing words.

"Lorcan, oh, Lorcan…"

"No. You do not get to grieve him now." I am wrenched up; the window's vivid colours mocking me as my vision greys. *Please let it stay grey.*

Lirrel shakes me and I hate the moan that leaves my mouth. He is correct. I have no right to grieve my husband. I relinquished that right when I put my trust in his future murderer. For one hundred years. Bitter, acrid truth fills me, but I do not have the strength to fight against him. He forces my face to his, anchoring me with fingertips as unyielding as clamps. I sense my shattered mind slipping away in tiny grains of sand, each one holding the hideous recollection of the last century.

"Now, Roselle. Now you shall submit to *me,*" Lirrel snarls and I flinch away from the monster in truth he has become. "I forsook all *for you.* Supping on base beings *for you.* So I could be worthy *for you.*"

How is this love? How can he purport to *love* me, when this only feels like hatred? Monstrous, insidious hatred. Perhaps, he contained his feelings for so long, that it morphed into something dark and wicked… or perhaps, it was I that had caused the darkness. Perhaps, it was always in me all along.

The clock on the tower strikes the first chime of midnight.

"I will not submit," I whisper, desperately railing against the deception in my mind. True grief fills me. Grief that I cannot avenge my family. That I could not free Lorcan. That all that awaits me now is to pursue him on to wherever blackened souls go when the door to this world closes on them. There will be no beckoning wing, no outstretched hand to welcome me home. Eternal damnation requires no such fanfare.

"You shall, Roselle, and you will *enjoy* it." Lirrel holds my face still and everything flashes before me as his mouth descends to mine, a flash of fangs behind his evil smile. *He* is the duke's true heir. Through and through.

As the clock continues to chime its slow tolling death knell, images of my family, dreams of Lorcan captured, the picture of his desperate eyes on mine as Lirrel slayed him assault my mind. It is all too much… and at the same time, not enough. I need to do this for me also. The realisation comes thick and fast. *I* deserve to be avenged too. The girl I was, the woman I should have become, the family I should have cherished… and the love, the love that I should have embraced.

I will not submit.

I have this one chance to take, and by darkness I *will* take it.

I rear back, using only what I have at my disposal;

the element of surprise. My motion pulls Lirrel off balance and I use it to my advantage. I extricate myself from his grasp and whirl around, running through the archway, seeking the wooden stake to wield it upon my foe.

I stop short; the scream pulling from my lips. All remnants of Lorcan—and the stake—are gone. *No*. My legs tremble as Lirrel catches ahold of me again.

I have no more weapons to employ. It was all in vain after all.

"Roselle, *stop resisting*. You have resisted me for a century, but I can make this so good, if you would only surrender." Lirrel strokes one long-nailed fingertip down my face, and I close my eyes. *Please madness take me. Take me before he does.*

"That's it. My Rose—" his words are abruptly cut off, and my eyes shoot open to see a strange look appear across his face, his features rippling and morphing. I shrink back. What is happening? "*No*," he utters. "Roselle…" His eyes claim mine one final time before he disappears and, save for the dust at my feet, it is as though he was never even here at all.

I stagger backwards, off-balance.

"That's 'my lady' to you," Lorcan says savagely. He stands in the place Lirrel just permanently vacated, stake in hand. He looks at me. "Hello, love, miss me?"

I stare at my husband. Hardly daring to believe that he is here, whole, and unharmed. "But, how?" I whisper, staring at the wooden stake, before raising my eyes to his beloved face.

He smiles and unbuttons his jacket, where a red stain mars his chest. "He missed," he says simply and I fall into his arms with a cry.

But as his lips descend towards mine, a pain sears through my own chest, and I gasp...I *gasp with breath*! And I feel a strange sensation in my chest, one that I never thought to feel again—my heartbeat. My own glorious, thundering, heartbeat. Is this real? Despite the strange sensations roving through my body, of my chest rising and falling rapidly, struggling to find its natural rhythm, I turn delighted eyes upon Lorcan. But he is pale—beyond his normal pale—and his hand moves up to press against his chest wound, *the wound not yet fully healed*. His hand comes away red.

Red upon red upon red.

The final chime sounds.

No. No. *No*.

He stumbles and I try to catch him but he is too heavy for me to now hold. I have only mortal strength, and that is weak at best, and I am still struggling under my own body trying to reclaim its mortal state, as my heart stutters and skips, trying to find its natural tempo.

My vision greys as Lorcan slumps to the floor, bringing me with him, but still I see the red pooling beneath him with every pump of his newly beating heart.

Immortality. Rebirth. Eternal death… oh what a fickle pendulum fate swings.

I try to scream, but I have no air. I have forgotten how to breathe it. *Lorcan*, my mind cries. *Somebody please help him.*

The grey turns to black as I feel gentle hands remove me from Lorcan's prone body. I no longer care about the lack of air, at the smothering sensation plaguing me. I willingly relinquish my tenuous hold on consciousness and float away into nothingness. Without Lorcan there is nothing. Even as we won, we lost. It *was* all in vain after all.

My eyes flutter open. Golden light spears through the room, and I reach out a hand as if I can touch it. The thought is a strange one. I have shied from the light for so long, how strange to actively seek its caress. But even as my hand trembles outstretched before me everything comes back in horrifying clarity and I let out a moan. *No.* I close my eyes tightly again, hoping that if I stay this way, the nightmare will cease.

"Roselle?" Ines' soothing voice comes from beside

me, followed by a soft hand on my brow. "Open your eyes. You are safe. You are alive… we are alive."

No, I am dead. Hell has finally claimed me. It is no more than I deserve. Without Lorcan, there is nought. "I have nothing to live for." My voice is raspy, as though it has not been used in an exceptionally long time. Or perhaps from the silent, gaping screams that were caught in my throat.

"Would you not live for me, my love?"

The deep voice stirs me, resurrects me back to life in truth.

I turn my head, hardly daring to believe it. The figure is shrouded in the sunlight pouring in through the tall arched windows. Perhaps this is heaven after all. "Lorcan?"

"Miss me?" he says tenderly, moving forward, and I take in his features, each and every beloved one of them. Even without the otherworldly enhancements he is just as handsome to me, even more so, because he is real, natural. As always intended. As I always saw him.

Ines rises from beside me and moves away towards the door. "I will return to speak with you soon," she says and leaves us.

Weakened or not, I push my way up from the bed, only to find myself ensconced in Lorcan's arms, fervent kisses being pressed to every part of my face.

"Rose, my Rose," he murmurs, then claims my lips with his.

I kiss him hungrily back as if it is the first time, and it is, for we are reborn, renewed into something true and pure. I clutch at him; he is all the air I need. But the reality is far different and soon we are breaking apart, chests heaving, loving smiles on our faces.

We return to the bed and he lies down next to me, eyes devouring every inch of my face.

"Ines saved you?" I ask.

He nods. "She arrived just in time. She overcame the transformation quicker than most and noticed our absence, just after Yves had been dealt with."

"I knew she was strong," I say, beyond thankful for her precipitous healing prowess. "I am so glad we were able to release her from this curse too. Will Duc LaCroix let her go?"

"Yes, he made us all a promise and he will honour it. He wants to prove that the European Court will be run with propriety. He has set up new laws and decrees, and any who do not abide by them will be dealt with harshly."

"So, that means…" I hardly dare voice it "…that we are all indeed free."

"Yes, my love, we have just left France. We are on our way back to England." Lorcan presses a kiss to my brow.

I hadn't even noticed the motion of the ship, but now I understand we are in a large cabin. "Will Ines stay in England?"

"No, she merely accompanies us to monitor us as we heal, but I have told her that my ship is at her disposal and will take her anywhere she wishes to go."

"Your ship?"

Lorcan nods. "I am a very wealthy man, my wife. George took care of my assets while I was... away." I lower my gaze in shame. For I was the one who had caused his lengthy absence.

Lorcan tenderly lifts my chin and looks deep into my eyes. "Do you know what first drew me to you, Roselle?" I mutely shake my head. "I saw a light inside you. It drew my dark moth to your flame. I could no more fight it, than whatever it was that drew you to me. And that light was the beacon of your goodness. *Of course* you would save your sister, Roselle, she was an innocent just as you were, just as Coralie and Mariette were. I would expect nothing less of you. I do not blame you." He strokes one finger along my cheek, holding my gaze. "*I do not blame you.*"

"But one hundred years, Lorcan. One hundred years I enforced our separation." Tears pool in my eyes.

"It was but the blink of an eye to immortals, my

love. Yes, we suffered, but it only made *this* worth fighting for."

"Oh, Lorcan, so you forgive me?"

"I was never truly angry at *you*. The monster inside me whispered vile things in my ear, until the red haze turned green with jealousy." He kisses me deep, proving just how deep the depth of his forgiveness ran. "But more importantly, you must forgive yourself," he says. "You were horribly deceived by one who had been concealing his true nature from you for a long time, but still you kept him at distance. Intrinsically you must have sensed it, and of course Yves orchestrated it all." His look is gentle and understanding. "You must forgive yourself, and relinquish it to the past, so that when we once again set foot on home soil, we will leave the shadows behind us and instead look to the light. Look to our future."

I place a soft hand against his cheek. "Our future is bright, my husband, and I want nothing more than to leave the shadows behind us."

"Then we will, my love. We will visit George, Marta, and Coralie, and then I shall purchase us a house to make our home in. Anywhere you desire."

I nestle in against his chest and listen in wonder to the strong thrum of his heart; an echo to my own, and smile. "Wherever you are, that, is home," I tell him.

His arms encircle me, and he lets out a sigh of contentment. "Home," he murmurs, and leans down to press a tender kiss to my lips.

EPILOGUE

The house behind me is filled with light and life.

Abandoning my own ancestral manor to the past—for it held too many dark memories, Lorcan found us a Scottish manor house near George and Marta's farmhouse.

I step out into the late January pre-dawn light. The frost glistens and crunches beneath my boots. I have witnessed another new year, another century turning, but this time I shall embrace it. Each second, each crystalline moment will be cherished. Savoured. For it shall be my last century. As it should be.

I toy with the opal amulet around my neck, the twin to the one Lorcan wears. Gifts from Ines before she carried on her own life's journey. The amulets shall repel any who seek to harm us and threaten our new life.

In my other hand I carry four white roses, and look towards the monument erected in our new home's gardens. Three angels stand together, the largest; a male, has his wings outstretched and curved around the two females; one older, one younger. I lay three of the roses at their feet.

Father. Mother. Nisette.

I shall honour them every day and live a life full of light and love. For far too long I existed in the shadows of their deaths, but no longer. I owe it to them, I owe it to myself, to embrace this gift I have been given. Their memory shall live on in me, and through the love they so abundantly bestowed upon me. It is only right that I pass that love on. To my husband, and any children we are blessed with.

"There you are, my love."

I turn at Lorcan's beloved voice, and dash away the single tear from my cheek.

He smiles tenderly down at me, before drawing me into his arms. I close my eyes against his chest and take comfort from his strong and steady heartbeat.

"You will make them proud, Rose," he says.

I ease back and look up at him. "And your mother would be so proud of you, Lorcan." I gesture to the marble bench in front of the monument. Another figure's wings encase the back of it, to look down benevolently at all who sit there and contemplate the stone tribute. I hand him the final rose, and he lays it reverently on the bench.

We share a look, piercing blue to bright green, and for one moment the past envelops us in a scudding mist. Lorcan smiles and the dark clouds vanish.

"All I wish now is to make you proud, my Rose, and be the best husband and, hopefully, father as I can be."

I smile back and rise up on my tiptoes to press a kiss to his lips. "Then why do we not make a start now?" I murmur against his lips.

I feel his lips curve against my own before he is claiming them in a searing kiss, one that weakens my knees and causes my heart to pound in a thrilling dance. He releases my lips only to claim my hand instead. He presses a lingering kiss to my palm, before he is linking my arm through his and leading me back to the house.

"Our future started the moment I laid my eyes upon you, Roselle," he says as we pause at the door. "But that was just a wish. But this, *this* is now the promise."

I lay my hand against his cheek. "Who needs forever?" I murmur, "When every moment with you shall be an eternity."

"True love transcends death, my love. We are testament to that."

"Then let us ascend to the next level and prove we

are worthy of such a gift." I take his hand and lead him through the quiet-yet-abundant halls and up to our chamber.

I will never tire of these moments where we pledge ourselves to each other over and over. Our love in a physical manifestation. So pure and bright I am surprised it does not light up the room as it lights me up from within.

If I have learned one thing from my past experience it is this: the sun always rises to sweep away the darkness. One must not fear the abyss, instead look for the creeping golden edge. A candle in the night. Seek it. It is always there. And for me, I found it burned deep within myself, all it took was some kindling to coax it into a flame.

Look for the light. Become the light. Never allow it to snuff out. Let it lead you to your heart's desire. Let love be your kindling, let life be your flame.

As Lorcan lowers me to the bed, the pale-blue light filtering in through the crystal clear windows turns golden.

Dawn approaches.

*A*cknowledgements

Love is never reserved simply for mortals. I truly believe it is the one thing we take with us when we die, so why not tell the imagined story of what happens afterwards. Does the manner of death create a monster? One that can no longer feel love? I was intrigued to find out, and so the tale of two lovers, fated to meet in unusual circumstances, was born. Faced with an impossible choice—which love pulled her the strongest—Roselle battled with her heart. But choosing the living over the already dead won out. But guilt, oh guilt, eats at us all. But love can revive even the darkest of graves, until hope, that ever-flickering flame fills it up.

And so, to my reasons for living: thank you, my beloved family, for always choosing me, loving me, lighting me up. I am rich beyond coin.

To Junie at Red Fox Creative. Thank you for creating the most stunning cover I have ever seen. You took my seeds of ideas and bloomed it into something beautiful…but with thorns and teeth.

Amanda, at Prose Perfect, thank you so much for your insightful edit and for championing my characters.

To Aerin, who read an early version, and loved it—I appreciate your support more than I can say. And to Julia, who once again came to my formatting rescue—thank you!

To all my writer friends on social media, thank you, always, for your continued encouragement. To my amazing ARC reader team, thank you for signing up and leaving wonderful early reviews—means the world!

And finally, to you, dearest reader, I hope you enjoyed this story and will think of love—and of hope—when you close your eyes.

Dawn approaches…

Estelle

About the Author

Estelle Tudor is an award-winning, multi-genre author from the land of myth and legend: Wales, where she lives with her husband, four children and doggy writing companion.

She loves to connect with her readers, and with fellow writers too, and can be found on:

X: @E_G_Tudor
Threads / Instagram: @from_the_garret_of_e_tudor
TikTok: @egtudor_author
Facebook: EG Tudor
Bluesky: @egtudor.bsky.social

You can also sign up to her newsletter below, for information on upcoming releases, giveaways, and writer life.
https://substack.com/@egtudor

Other Books

The 'Through the Fairy Door' series, Fantasy Portal
books for MG readers, written under
ESTELLE GRACE TUDOR:

OCTAVIA BLOOM AND THE MISSING KEY (2020)
BEATRICE BLOOM AND THE STAR CRYSTAL (2020)
MARTHA BLOOM AND THE GLASS COMPASS
(2021)
FELICITY BLOOM AND THE GOLDEN ARROW
(2021)
OTTO BLOOM AND THE ENCHANTED COIN (2021)

The 'Fated Partners' trilogy, a Romantasy series for
Upper YA readers, written under E.G. TUDOR:

WHERE FATE WHISPERS (2022)
WHERE DESTINY LIES (2023)
WHERE HOPE BURNS (to be published)

The 'Regency meets Fantasy' series, Paranormal
Regency Romance books for Adult readers:

MASQUERADE FALL (2023)
THE LEGEND OF ANGELHAVEN (2023)

THE SWORD AND THE STONE HEART (2023)
SYMPHONY OF ANGELS (to be published)
TEARS FROM HEAVEN (to be published)

A 'Standalone' Contemporary Romance for Adult readers:

EXCAVATING THE BURIED HEART (2024)

The 'Cupids & Cocktails' series, Cosy Fantasy Romance for Adult readers:

LOVE STRUCK (2025)

An historical romantic adventure for Adult readers, published by LUNA EDEN PUBLISHING:

ARCHAEOLOGY OF THE STARS (JULY 2025)

Available in multiple formats from all online book stores.

Request at your local library too.